The TRUTH ABOUT ABOUT Peacock BLUE

ROSANNE HAWKE

The TRUTH ABOUT Peacock BLUE

ALLEN&UNWIN
SYDNEY · MELBOURNE · AUCKLAND · LONDON

The Truth about Peacock Blue is based on Rosanne Hawke's short story, 'Just a Schoolgirl', in Kennedy, M. (ed.), *Reaching Out: Stories of Hope*, Sydney: HarperCollins, 2013.

First published by Allen & Unwin in 2015

Allen & Unwin – Australia
83 Alexander Street, Crows Nest NSW 2065, Australia
Phone: (61 2) 8425 0100
Email: info@allenandunwin.com
Web: www.allenandunwin.com

Allen & Unwin – UK
c/o Murdoch Books,
Erico House, 93–99 Upper Richmond Road, London SW15 2TG, UK
Phone: (44 20) 8785 5995
Email: info@murdochbooks.co.uk
Web: www.allenandunwin.com
Murdoch Books is a wholly owned division of Allen & Unwin Pty Ltd

A Cataloguing-in-Publication entry is available from the National Library of Australia www.trove.nla.gov.au. A catalogue record for his book is available from the British Library.

ISBN (AUS) 978 1 74331 994 9
ISBN (UK) 978 1 74336 763 6

Cover and text design by Debra Billson
Cover photos: portrait of girl by Getty Images/azgAr Donmaz; additional images by Shutterstock and CanStock Photo
Set 11 on 14 pt Legacy in by Midland Typesetters, Australia

Printed in Australia by McPherson's Printing Group

10 9 8 7 6 5 4 3 2 1

For Asia Bibi and all those unjustly accused

We must accept finite disappointment,
but never lose infinite hope.
MARTIN LUTHER KING JR

Hope means hoping when everything seems hopeless.
GILBERT K CHESTERTON (1874–1936)

Act justly, love mercy, and walk humbly with God.
MICAH 6:8

CHAPTER

1

The night Ijaz died, I didn't even dream of him. I thought I would have known, but I woke in the morning to the sound of my mother's wailing. He had died in his sleep. Some say that is the best way to die but he was only fifteen.

I remember the funeral as if it were a black-and-white silent movie. Everyone in the village rallied for it and other relatives began arriving in the afternoon. In the house Ammi cried over the coffin; I saw her open mouth, the way she shook, but I couldn't comfort her. She even pulled open the lid in front of everyone and dragged him to her breast, banging him on the back, rocking back and forth.

I wanted to say, *Wake up, Ijaz!* In my head I was shaking him but I was far away, watching as if from a high cloud. Maybe tomorrow life would be normal and I'd return to earth, to feel again.

Ijaz and I were close. He was often inside due to his breathing and, since Abba was a tailor, he had taught him how to sew shalwar qameezes, the baggy trousers and long shirts everyone wears. I embroidered around the necklines and cuffs. Our grandmother Dadi-ji had taught me the Punjabi phulkari designs using a simple satin stitch, even though she couldn't see well enough to embroider clothes anymore. I loved the way coloured thread could make a garden of flowers appear on a qameez.

Ijaz and I were a good team; even in church he played the tabla, a hand drum, with our cousin Sammy while I sang. Why couldn't he have stayed alive? It wouldn't have been any trouble at all for God to fix his lungs.

Our family from further south in Pakistan came on buses for the funeral: our cousin Barakat, with whom Ijaz used to correspond on Facebook, and his two sisters. Ijaz and I first met him after the big monsoon flood when I was ten. Our mud houses didn't hold up against the raging river and the village had to be rebuilt. Uncle Yusef from Australia came to help, even though he knew nothing about building. He paid for cement so the school and church would be pukka. A flood would never dissolve them again.

I followed the procession to church; Sammy and Barakat were carrying Ijaz's coffin along with Abba and my uncles. Inside the church, there were prayers about the surety of eternal life. We all knew where Ijaz was but that didn't make his passing any easier to bear. Later at the cemetery Colonel Rafique and Mrs Rafique, in whose house Ammi worked, arrived and stood near Dadi-ji, as if they, also, were grandparents. Sammy stood beside me. He didn't hug me or hold my hand like Ijaz would have – we were too old for that now, for he was my cousin, and in our culture cousins are allowed to marry. Barakat was probably the type of boy that my parents would consider when they arranged my marriage, but Sammy? He was more like an older brother to me.

So many of Ijaz's friends came but I hardly spoke to anyone, wishing that it would all be over soon. I kept wiping my eyes with a tissue under my glasses.

My closest cousin Hadassah was away, and with my other cousins helping to serve food, I was bereft.

Uncle Yusef, Aunty Noori and Maryam had trouble getting a flight quickly from Australia, so they arrived a few days after the funeral. When I first saw Maryam in our house I fell into her arms and sobbed. She was older than me and so confident and beautiful in her Australian-styled shalwar qameez.

'I'm glad you came.'

'I'm so sorry, Aster,' she said.

I nodded but I couldn't stop the tears. Ammi was crying on Aunty Noori's shoulder too.

That afternoon Maryam and I went for a walk to the canal to bring our buffalo Gudiya home.

'I haven't had anyone close to me die, not since Dada-ji when I was little. I can't imagine how you feel, how to help . . .' Maryam's voice trailed away.

'It's good that you came. That helps.' I turned to her.

'Dadi-ji told me a story this morning. Did you know she had a brother who died in the Partition?'

Maryam shook her head.

'She's never gotten over it.'

'Never?'

'Nay, but she said she healed around it like a wound, and he's still inside her heart.' I sighed, blinking the tears away again. 'Ijaz is like that – he's still with me.'

I rolled my lips together to stop them from trembling and Maryam took my hand. We walked without talking until we saw the canal. Gudiya was trudging around the well in her yoke, oblivious to the cataclysmic shift in our lives.

'Have you heard from Hadassah?' Maryam suddenly asked. Hadassah had moved away from the village during the year.

I shook my head. 'This was where it happened.' I pointed at the wheatfield. 'A few months later she left to do a tailoring course.'

Hadassah had gone without saying goodbye, just like Ijaz. Then I felt ashamed. How could Ijaz have said goodbye? Perhaps Hadassah couldn't either.

CHAPTER

2

It had taken only that morning almost a year before to shift the way I viewed the world, to see the danger we lived with daily. I was not yet thirteen and still thought life consisted of cricket and songs. I had woken Dadi-ji so she could start making chapattis. Then I put our clay water pot on my head to walk to the canal just like Dadi-ji used to do years before.

I loved my village with its square mud houses and high walls and I enjoyed walking alone to fetch water early. It was a good time to think because I didn't have to look after the little cousins or do jobs for Ammi. Soon the adults would be in the fields working for the landlord and after breakfast I'd go to the village school with Hadassah. But for now it was peaceful.

I passed the tin oil drum where Hadassah, Sammy and I had played cricket the evening before. Ijaz had joined in, but he was soon puffed out. His breathing made strange noises when it was laboured.

'Hey, whistler,' Sammy called, 'why don't you bat instead? I'll run for you.'

We four were like a club even though Ijaz and Sammy had started high school in the nearby town.

We had an argument over the tin drum. I was bowling, Ijaz hit the tennis ball and Sammy lobbed it to me. It came whizzing towards me. I'd learned to catch it while swinging my arms back so it wouldn't jar my hands, and I threw it at the drum. Bang!

'Out!' I shouted, with my finger in the air like they did on TV.

'Hoi!' Ijaz called. 'If the drum was the right height I wouldn't be out.'

Sammy had the hugest smile. He came to my rescue even though he didn't need to.

'Then find a smaller wicket, bhai!' He always called Ijaz 'brother' though they were cousins. Sammy would do anything for me, like buying toffees from the village shop and giving me half. Sammy's mud-brick house and ours were close together and we shared the same courtyard, and hens and goats and Gudiya the buffalo. We even shared the cooking.

Gudiya was already blindfolded, turning the water wheel. We called her Gudiya because her big brown eyes and black eyelashes were like a doll's. Water was pouring into the canal, but no one was there. Who had brought her down to start work?

As I held the pot in the canal to fill, I heard a scream. I dropped the pot and followed the sounds to the edge of the wheatfield. And there I saw Hadassah on the ground, struggling. A boy much bigger than her was holding her arms above her head; another boy had his back to me. He was telling Hadassah to shut up or he'd cut her face. The first boy saw me standing there, gaping.

'Wah, here's another – it's our lucky day.'

I did the first thing that came to my head: I yelled for my father even though the village was too far away for him to hear.

'Abba, help!' I glanced behind me, wishing he were there.

The boys ran, one tying up his shalwar. Maybe they thought Abba was with me.

I rushed forward.

'Hadassah? Are you all right?' I stopped when I saw her bloodied nose and face. She didn't answer but I managed to help her stand. Her shalwar had blood on them and she had trouble moving her legs but we hobbled to her house on the other side of the village. Her older brothers were already out searching for her.

Aunty Feebi, her mother, was in tears. 'Where did you find her?'

'Near the wheatfield.'

Her face closed in on itself when she saw the state Hadassah was in. She ushered Hadassah inside but she sent me home.

The adults tried to keep it quiet but I heard Ammi telling Abba, 'It was the landlord's sons who attacked her.'

Silence. Then my father said, 'Who would believe us? In the eyes of the police she would be the criminal. We must do nothing this time.' There was another pause. 'Remember what happened to the village near Lahore? Those Christians complained about their girls being attacked and the whole village was burned. Khuda in heaven will be the judge of those boys.'

My mother was silent, but Ijaz whispered to me, 'If anyone harmed you I'd kill them.'

I opened my eyes wide at my gentle brother. 'Then you'd end up in jail. They'd torture you.'

He gave me a playful punch. I jumped on him and in no time he was coughing and asking for mercy. Yet even though I didn't understand the full extent of what had happened, the image of Hadassah bloodied and struggling caught in my heart and Abba's words of burning villages frightened me.

After Hadassah's 'accident', as Ammi referred to it, we girls collected water in pairs. If a brother was available, he came too; Sammy never needed cajoling to walk with me to the well. I became wary and never again did I go down an empty lane alone, enjoying the peace of the early morning.

The real Hadassah disappeared inside herself. We had a special bond because of our names. We were both named after the same Jewish queen: Hadassah bore her Hebrew name and I was given her Persian one. Hadassah said it made us sisters.

But she never played cricket with us again. She didn't even come shopping.

Three months after the incident her mother told us Hadassah had a good opportunity to study women's tailoring in a village south of Lahore. 'She will be away for more than a year.'

Hadassah took the train from Rawalpindi. Nothing like that had ever happened in our village and when I asked Ammi about it she closed her lips and said not a word.

Hadassah didn't email me to explain or even send a message on Facebook.

Our guests must have stayed a week after Ijaz's funeral but everything was a blur. Maryam and her parents finally returned to Australia and I tried to live as I did before Ijaz died, but it wasn't the same. I felt enveloped in a fog, mechanically doing my jobs and going to school but I couldn't remember what I'd learned or where I'd put things. I retreated deep inside myself like Hadassah had, and for the first time I understood what she must have been feeling: she too had been grieving. When Sammy's little siblings wanted stories and songs I didn't have the energy, nor did I want to play games with Sammy. I certainly did not feel like using Ijaz's profile on Facebook.

Christmas was unbearable without Ijaz. Abba was brave enough to preach in church, but I couldn't sing. Every Christmas song reminded me of Ijaz and me singing together, of him sewing me a dupatta, a scarf with a peacock design as a gift, him praying and reading me books.

Once the Christmas holidays were over the village teacher, Miss Saima, visited my parents. After all the pre-liminaries – savouries, chai and sweet biscuits – she finally told us why she came.

'Aster is a talented student, Pastor Suleiman. She could hold her own in the Government Girls High School.'

'That would be expensive,' Ammi said.

'There would be many opportunities for Aster with more education,' Miss Saima said gently.

Then Abba said, right in front of me, 'We have our eye on opportunities for Aster. Boys in our family in other villages have good jobs now and we can marry Aster to one of them.'

Miss Saima chewed her bottom lip. What did she expect? No girls from our village went to the high school in town. I would be expected to marry and raise the boys who went to high school.

She tried again. 'I am from a village like this one and my parents sent me to high school so I could have a career. Now I help support them.'

Abba turned to me. I saw the speculation in his gaze but I wondered if Miss Saima's seed would take root. Abba knew a lot about the world; he was educated in a Bible school and preached in church. He even let me teach the little kids Bible stories in kids' church, but he hadn't before thought I could be like Miss Saima.

Miss Saima continued, 'Aster is truly intelligent and could be a teacher.'

When she left, Abba closed his eyes momentarily. I knew he was praying. His faith was simple, yet firm. Would mine ever be that strong?

When he opened his eyes he raised his eyebrows at Ammi and she nodded.

'Aster,' he said, 'it is a good idea. In April when the new school year starts you will go to high school in the place of Ijaz. You will have a career.'

The rest of his thoughts were unspoken but I understood. I was to be a breadwinner to help the family until I could be married. Sons look after their parents and single sisters, and in my village it was unusual for Abba to think this way about me. Parents who only had daughters didn't turn them into boys – they hoped for early marriages.

That was the moment my life irrevocably changed. Not only did I become an only child at the age of thirteen and a girl grieving for an attentive older brother, but I was now the hope of my family.

CHAPTER

3

The rickshaw idled, putt-putt-putt, like a rich person's lawnmower spewing black smoke outside our house. Abba was taking me to high school. Although he was a tailor he drove a rickshaw taxi when he didn't have sewing jobs, so he'd find taxi work during the day until it was time to collect me. Dadi-ji smiled while Ammi kissed me and handed me my lunch: a rolled chapatti filled with leftover curry, wrapped in a chapatti cloth. I put it in my backpack and climbed into the seat behind Abba.

'Wait! Uncle-ji, wait for me!'

I grinned at Sammy running towards us, his bag banging on his back.

When he pulled himself into the rickshaw beside me, I asked, 'What makes you think you can travel to school with me? Why aren't you catching the bus on the main road?' I moved my backpack to the floor between my feet.

He poked me with his elbow. 'We are the only two from

the village attending high school at the moment, so why shouldn't I beg a ride with you?'

Abba glanced at us in the rear-vision mirror, amused.

Sammy sat with his bag on his lap and gave me an approving grin. 'Nice uniform.'

It was my turn to elbow him. But he was right, I had dressed carefully in the Government Girls High School uniform: white shalwar and blue qameez, a white serviceable cotton dupatta, scarf and black shoes. Abba had made the shalwar qameez for me and I'd sewn the hems. My hair was in a neat black plait tied with a blue ribbon. Only girls fairer than me were called beautiful but my nose and mouth could have been considered pretty, if my eyes weren't so huge and dark. My glasses made them even more pronounced.

At least I had glasses, as Abba often pointed out. He took me to the eye doctor at Taxila after I had cooked the rice one night. As he ate Ijaz had screwed up his nose. 'The cumin hasn't made the rice taste better.'

I'd cried, 'But I haven't added cumin,' and inspected a spoonful. 'Hoi, it's mice dirt!'

Ijaz spat out his mouthful, spraying my plate as well. It took years for the teasing to cease.

'So, my beti is going to high school.' My father shouted it above the noise of the motor. He was proud of me and I grinned at his reflection in the mirror.

I watched the fields fly by, the buffaloes ambling, farm workers walking to the fields with their scythes over their shoulders. It was spring and hay was being cut. A flock of goats barricaded the road and Abba changed gears to inch past so as not to frighten them.

'You mustn't be late on the first day,' Abba shouted into the rear-vision mirror.

I grinned at Sammy. I was more excited than I showed, but hesitant too. Abba thought school was just about arithmetic, writing and exams but I suspected it wouldn't be easy changing from the village school to the big high school.

'Do your best and Khuda will do the rest' was one of his stock statements. But I knew there would be forty girls or more in my class who I didn't know and who wouldn't know me.

He dropped Sammy at the boys' high school first and when we arrived at the girls' school, Abba took me straight to the principal's office.

'Welcome to our school.' Mrs Iqbal smiled at me. 'You will learn well and make many pleasant memories here.'

Then Abba voiced our concern. 'We are a Masihi family—'

Mrs Iqbal cut in, 'She will be expected to take all the same subjects as the other girls, but she will be free to follow her Christian faith.'

Abba relaxed. 'Accha, good.' Then he stood. 'I will leave her with you. Each day I will collect her at the gate.'

Mrs Iqbal inclined her head. 'A good arrangement.'

I didn't look at him as he left for fear I would lose my nerve. As if she knew Mrs Iqbal said briskly, 'I will take you to your class now. It is one of our best.'

When we walked in the girls stood. They had been quietly working in exercise books. There were so many of them, they seemed like a forest.

'Year Eights, this is a new classmate, Aster Suleiman Masih.'

By telling them my full name Mrs Iqbal had told them I was different from them: Masih means Christ.

The teacher showed me a seat by a girl whose ruler bore the name Rabia. And so the day began. At recess Rabia faithfully took me down a long verandah and showed me where the latrine was at the end of the building and where to buy snacks. Then she took me to a covered area between two buildings where girls were eating and laughing.

'Have you lived in the town long?' I asked.

'All my life.' She regarded me as if gauging what to say next. 'Why didn't you attend the Government Primary School?'

How to answer that? 'I live in a village and I attended the school there. But my parents decided to send me to high school here since we don't have one.'

She nodded. I supposed that all these girls came from families with enough money to educate the girls as well as the boys. I wouldn't even be here if Ijaz were still alive.

We were returning to our room when two girls from the class stood in our path.

'Do your parents sweep the streets and gutters like most Christians?' one said.

I flinched at the scorn in her tone. Rabia told me her name later: Saleema. I had no answer, for my Dalit great-grandfather, Shahbaz, had indeed been a sweeper of the streets, before an Englishman told him he didn't have to wait centuries to work his way to heaven.

'And their latrines?' another sneered. 'Watch yourself, Rabia.' She barely suppressed a snort. 'You don't want to catch a disease.'

'Ji, yes,' Saleema didn't hide her giggle, 'you might grow ugly overnight.'

Rabia shifted her feet uncomfortably and the girls moved on. I didn't know what to say and neither did she. I hoped it wouldn't stop her talking to me. No one else had even said 'salaam'.

The worst lesson of the day was Islamiyat. The teacher, Mrs Abdul, saw my name on the roll and narrowed her gaze at me. She didn't welcome me to the class, but recited a verse from the Qur'an and asked me to repeat it. It was unfamiliar to me.

'Allah . . .' I began, then faltered.

'Not listening, Aster?'

A few of the girls sniggered but Rabia stared at the desk. The lesson didn't get any better from there.

When Abba picked me up, he asked, 'And how did your day go?'

By his tone he was expecting me to chat excitedly about how grateful I was for this wonderful opportunity. 'Don't ask,' was all I said.

He looked at my face in the rear-vision mirror. 'Beti, you will need to prove your love. The girls will like you when they see how genuine you are.'

I blew out a slow breath as we stopped at the boys' high school to pick up Sammy. The girls may not be the biggest problem. I had a feeling that Mrs Abdul would never warm to me.

CHAPTER

4

Abba's favourite motto was 'Do not fear'. He would say, 'We must love at all times, beti. There is no fear in love.' It was difficult at times to live up to Abba's expectations. 'Not mine,' he'd say. 'Khuda's.'

How not to fear? Didn't we all feel fear when Hadassah was attacked, that it could happen again? When Shahbaz Bhatti, the minister for minorities, was killed for supporting those accused of blasphemy, weren't we afraid our village would be attacked next by Muslim extremists? When Salman Taseer, the governor of Punjab, was assassinated for attempting to reform the blasphemy law, Abba prayed constantly for our family, that repercussions wouldn't fall on minority groups like us.

I didn't tell my parents I was afraid to return to school and I didn't have Hadassah to confide in, nor could I write to her. No one would tell me where she was.

I told Sammy instead. 'Most of the subjects are fine, but

Arabic and Islamiyat are difficult. And the teacher is aggressive. The girls look down their noses at me.' I thought of Rabia. 'Most of them . . .' I grimaced.

'Maybe you'll get used to it, maybe not. But think of the education you are getting. You'll be the most intelligent of us all.' He laughed.

Why did I bother to confide in him? For sympathy? I thought of Saleema. How could I describe her vindictiveness?

Sammy saw my hesitation and his tone changed. 'Aster, it won't be easy at first. The kids are fed such lies about us, that we worship three gods and swap wives like Americans. But once you make a friend, it will get easier.'

I gazed at him, desolate. I couldn't imagine it.

'My dost Ahmed? We became friends over a game of soccer. Then cricket. Now all the boys like me.'

I despaired. I would have loved to play cricket or soccer but there were no girls' sports at the school. Sports would encourage girls like Saleema to be fair-minded.

It was as if Sammy could follow my thoughts. Maybe he had been through more than he let on, for he said, 'Don't let a few people ruin your day. There will be many others who are willing to be kind once they see you are human.'

He leaned closer. 'You are a caring, sensitive girl, even though you're noisy and as blind as a bat.'

I dug him in the ribs.

'You'll get a friend soon, but don't wait for it to happen – make a friend.' He pulled a stupid face and in no time had me laughing. Sammy was good for that. If we hadn't grown up together I wondered if he would have been chosen for me. We got on so well.

Then I thought of Barakat. At Ijaz's funeral he was weeping and kept glancing at me. He was even good-looking like Ijaz; it would be no hardship to be married to him. I berated myself. His parents would be thinking of someone fairer than me. Someone with better eyesight who could see if the mice had broken into the rice bag.

School on Monday didn't improve. Rabia said 'salaam' but that was all. I sat at my desk dreading what would come.

The maths teacher entered. Miss Rehmat was young. She was also different from Mrs Abdul. She wore a dupatta but I hadn't seen her in a burqa like Mrs Abdul. She put a maths problem on the board. 'Please copy this into your exercise books.'

She walked around the class as we each solved it. I was surprised: usually teachers remained at the front. If they wanted to check our work they asked students to bring it. The problem wasn't difficult, yet she paused slightly behind my chair before walking back to the front.

She spun to face us. 'Aster.'

A feeling of horror spread upward from my belly.

'Would you care to solve the problem on the board for us all to see?'

I hesitated. What if she showed everyone that this was how *not* to do it? That would give Saleema more fuel to burn me.

'Just as you did in your notebook.' Miss Rehmat held out the chalk.

Rabia tipped her chin at the board and grinned. I walked slowly to the front, planning my first move. When I reached the board, I didn't have to think, I just copied in a few strokes what I had in my exercise book.

'This is the best way to do this type of problem,' Miss Rehmat said to the class.

There was a silence so heavy my legs almost gave way. She turned to me. 'Where did you learn your maths?'

'In my village school—' I began.

There were sniggers but Miss Rehmat glanced up and they stopped. I could have added how Ijaz gave me extra problems from his textbook when I had finished my own. I returned to my desk but caught Saleema's baleful gaze on me. With my heart sinking I realised Miss Rehmat's actions hadn't helped me any.

The English teacher was efficient, yet she put aside time to read to us. Abba had encouraged Ijaz to read in English and so I did also. Even some of our church songs were in English.

Miss Saed-Ulla read from *To Kill a Mockingbird*. 'Yes, this is an American book, but it did more to change attitudes about race than any other work of art in the twentieth century,' she said. 'We must let art be free to cross cultural and racial borders, especially those of distrust and intolerance.'

I stared at her with interest. Abba had said a similar thing about our faith: 'Being Masihi has nothing to with other countries but everything to do with our own relationship with Khuda.'

I began to look forward to English lessons. It was only Mrs Abdul's classes I dreaded and she had two periods every day: Arabic and Islamiyat. However hard I tried, my efforts in class never pleased her. She always reprimanded me. It was as if she knew I would get it wrong.

That Monday was the start of how she would always treat me. She called me to the front to check my homework book.

'You didn't do your work correctly, you stupid girl.' She glared at me. 'This is not good enough!' She threw the book at me; it hit the side of my head and my glasses fell to the floor. I scrambled for them.

When I stood, I said, 'Ji, miss, I did my best,' careful to be respectful.

I wanted to explain that I didn't grow up with Arabic, had never heard my father read the Qur'an aloud like other girls in the class. I was told different stories in Punjabi. Even my Injeel, my New Testament, was printed in Urdu.

'Your best is not enough, lazy girl. If you did your homework properly you would understand the lesson today.'

A few of the girls smirked as I returned to my desk, blinking too much. When I glanced up I noticed Rabia watching me with pity in her eyes.

It wasn't fair. I looked like them, only with slightly darker skin from my Dalit great-grandfather. I also wore a scarf like them. But they knew I was different in a way that went much deeper than my skin colour. I even had a name no other Muslim girl in the class had. Imagine if they knew I was named after a Jewish queen.

At lunchtime, Rabia sought me out in the covered area. I was eating leftover curry and rice from my three tiered-lunch tin. 'I'm sorry about what happened in class. Mrs Abdul will always be upset with you because you are the only Masihi and you haven't said the Kalimah.'

I swallowed my mouthful in a rush. 'The principal assured my father I wouldn't have to convert to attend school.'

Ijaz had told me Yesu Masih, Jesus Christ, is in the Qur'an, but Mrs Abdul never mentioned Him. She didn't try to find common ground for me like Ijaz's teacher had for him.

'I wish I didn't have to do Islamiyat – it's mostly Arabic and I will never manage the answers that Mrs Abdul wants.'

Rabia sat beside me. 'Why don't you say the first Kalimah for her? All you have to do is state: "There is no god but God and Muhammad is the messenger of God". Say it in Arabic and it won't mean a thing. Then she will stop bothering you. You'll be her special project.'

My breaths came short and fast.

'I couldn't. Certainly, I believe there is only one God, but I can't say that about Muhammad. Yesu Masih is the last Prophet. He's the son of—'

'Chup! Quiet!' Rabia cut me off and checked behind us. 'Don't say that here. It will be misunderstood and you could be accused of blasphemy!'

'But I'm only saying what I believe. I'm not meaning to blaspheme.'

'All the same, be more careful.'

I decided the kindness in her eyes was genuine. 'Why do you care?'

Rabia opened her mouth. She formed two words, 'My father . . .' and then stopped, as if in horror that she had spoken at all.

The bell rang and as we returned to class I wondered what she almost said.

CHAPTER

5

Sunday night was our village church service. We had one on Friday night too but on Sunday evenings the children and youth led the service. This was when I missed Ijaz the most. He had been a good speaker like Abba, despite his coughing fits, and his prayers had made me think I could see into heaven. All I'd have to do was put my arm up to touch the sky and I'd reach it as if the space between heaven and earth was thinner there. It was easier to believe when Ijaz was alive.

That Sunday, we had a guest speaker. He was a young doctor, recently graduated. He brought his keyboard and Sammy played the tabla for him.

I'd never heard a voice as rich as Dr Amal's. He sang a song he had written called 'Umeed'. It was about hope and I felt my spirit lift slightly.

'Life may be hard for us,' he said in his talk afterwards, 'but Khuda will always give us strength to be victorious.

Always live according to his will and be faithful in whatever situation we find ourselves.'

I was still grumpy – I bet he hadn't met Mrs Abdul – but the grumpiness was lessening. When I stood up to lead the singing again with Sammy, Dr Amal joined in. Afterwards we had chai served from a hotpot and he spoke to me.

'You are Ijaz's sister?'

I nodded, nonplussed and inexplicably shy.

'He was my friend on Facebook. I was very sorry about his passing.'

I realised then he would have been at the funeral; I'd hardly noticed anything that day. I inclined my head and murmured, 'Shukriya, thank you.'

'You and your friends can follow me on Facebook too. I post video clips of my songs, so you can learn new ones.'

I brightened. That would be fun and I could teach them to the fellowship on Sunday nights.

'Shukriya. That is very kind.'

'I have a heart for these little Christian villages,' he said, 'striving to survive without being engulfed by Islam.'

That night I went on Facebook for the first time since Ijaz died. It had been six months. We had a computer in our house and our neighbours often came to use it. At times, our house was like an internet café, especially at Christmas. When Ammi was working at the Rafiques' house, I made the chai for any uncles and aunts who wanted to send emails. I didn't bother for the cousins.

'No games,' Abba said. 'The computer is only for designated homework and important emails.'

Less people used our computer once Uncle Ibrahim bought one when Sammy began high school.

I didn't have a Facebook profile as Ijaz had let me send messages on his to Hadassah and Maryam. Ijaz's wall had been silent for so long that I decided to take over his profile. Maybe I should have started my own, but I would have quick access to his friends' list, plus the doctor, and in a warm way it made me feel Ijaz was still here.

Was that so bad? Just as my finger hovered to click I thought about it some more. Ijaz would have had male 'friends' and they would see everything I wrote, plus they would know it wasn't Ijaz. I needed a new profile image.

My favourite bird was the peacock. I painted and drew them, even embroidered them with the material held up close to my glasses. I scanned in a painting I'd done in a sketchbook, then inserted it in Ijaz's profile. I unticked Ijaz's personal information and typed in 'A Peacock Admirer'. The peacock materialised with its vibrant blue feathers and hundreds of green eyes. I used the head and blue chest as the profile image and the green-eyed tail spread like a fan for the cover image.

What could I call myself? Not my real name in case Abba wasn't pleased. Blue was my favourite colour so I typed in Peacock Blue instead of Ijaz's name. Then I sent a message to Sammy.

MESSAGES

Peacock Blue Salaam, guess who this is?

Sammy Ibrahim You gave me a fright. I thought it was Ijaz haunting me. Is that you, Aster?

Peacock Blue Ji, but call me Peacock Blue on the wall.

I searched for Hadassah; I was sure she'd had a profile, but it was gone.

Then I found the doctor's page. Yes, we were already friends. There were so many video clips, not only of his songs, but of other bands too. I found the one called 'Umeed' that he sang at our church. There he was, standing at his keyboard singing. I clicked it to play.

> *In times of hopelessness*
> *You are my living hope*
> *In the darkness, You are my vibrant light*
> *My faith, hope and destination is You,*
> *O Yesu Masih, only You.*

MESSAGES

Maryam Yusef Hi, Peacock Blue. Is that you, Aster? Isn't this Ijaz's profile?

Peacock Blue Salaam, Maryam. Ji, it's Aster. I wasn't sure how to set one up of my own since Ijaz always let me send messages on his – just easier for me this way. I wanted to see some music videos of a friend of his so I'll share them with you.

Maryam Yusef It's wonderful to hear from you at last. Are you feeling better?

Peacock Blue Better than when you saw me last. I'm going to high school now. Middle school, really, I'm in Year 8.

Maryam Yusef That's great. I started uni this year in February. I'm studying teaching. The first few months have been good so far.

Peacock Blue That's what I'd like to study. I have 3 years of school, 2 years of college. Then I'll be able to teach. Though school is not as good as Abba thinks it is.

Maryam Yusef Why do you say that?

Peacock Blue Some of the girls see me as Christian scum, I think, but the worst is the Islamiyat teacher. She gets angry with me very easily.

Maryam Yusef Why don't you tell the principal?

Peacock Blue I think the teacher would be worse.

Maryam Yusef She shouldn't be allowed to get away with it.

Peacock Blue Thanks for caring. What else is new?

Maryam Yusef I'll be 18 soon and I'll have my Ps, my driving licence.

Peacock Blue Wah, I can't imagine that. Just to have a career and help my family is a big thing for me. Is all your family well?

Maryam Yusef Ji, all are well. Abu is still working as a dentist. Lovely autumn weather here in Adelaide. You must come to visit.

Peacock Blue How I wish.

Maryam Yusef Nothing is impossible.

Peacock Blue So Abba says. Give my salaam to Uncle Yusef and Aunty Noori and all your family. Khuda Hafiz, God keep you safe.

Maryam Yusef Khuda Hafiz.

CHAPTER

6

On Friday afternoon, our chutti from school, I went with Ammi to Mrs Rafique's house. I loved going there when I was younger. Mrs Rafique gave me embroidery threads and paints. It was there that I first developed my obsession for peacocks. Mrs Rafique raised them and sold the chicks, usually to other rich people so they could have peacocks gracing their mowed lawns. At dusk she shut the hens and chicks in a huge cage she called an aviary and the peacocks roosted in the trees.

Mrs Rafique had an English-style garden with a high wall and during the day the birds strutted under the trees. Her gardener looked so old he must have tended the garden during the Raj. Mr Rafique had been a colonel in the Pakistani army and they were both fond of my mother. She did their washing, ironing, mending and cooking.

Abba even made any clothes they needed, though Mrs Rafique bought her best clothes in fancy emporiums in

Islamabad. I'd never seen such a shop, though I'd heard one was being built in town. It was Mrs Rafique who paid for Ijaz's medicine. Even though they were Muslims they gave Ijaz and me new clothes each Christmas, and at Eid after Ramadan they gave us food and gifts.

When I was born Mrs Rafique brought food into the hospital for Ammi and a whole box of clothes for me. At Ijaz's funeral you'd have thought they were his grandparents.

'Aster, how lovely to see you.'

'Salaam, Aunty-ji.'

'How is school?'

She was so interested that I wondered if they paid part of the fees. I made an effort and told her I had a friend called Rabia (possibly not true) and that I enjoyed all my studies (definitely not true).

How could I tell her about the discrimination I felt? She'd probably think I'd imagined it. Someone like her would never have felt any discrimination in her life.

I took my sketchbook and sat in the garden to draw the birds. I was always looking for ideas to embroider. I had made Mrs Rafique peacock cushion covers for her lounge room, using colours she liked, maroon and green, but I sewed peacock blue in as well. I couldn't help it, since it's my favourite colour. It was a wrench giving them away so I made a replica for myself.

One bird called Neelum (not very imaginative, since neela means blue) swished his tail past my legs.

'You never open your fan when I want you to, Neelum.'

He turned about and showed me his brown and white back feathers. A fossicking hen pecked the ground nearby, taking no notice of either of us. He saw the hen and gave his haunting cry. Then he raised his tail but he wouldn't face me. Every time I stood up to sketch him from the front, he turned the other way and shook his back feathers at me.

'Neelum, behave. Don't you know by now that the hen doesn't think you're amazing at all? Only I do, so show me your fan.'

And just then he did – he faced me and gave me the full benefit of his raised tail. I would never grow used to his display. What a perfect circle of blue and green, and hundreds of eyes like teardrops. Some people think the eyes on the tail are a sign of evil and won't take the feathers inside, but I didn't think there was anything evil about Neelum.

Just then one of Mrs Rafique's grandchildren, Rahul, ran up to me. He was a polite boy with fair skin, who always wore clean, expensive clothes. This time he didn't clamour for a story.

'Nana-ji wants to see you, Asti.'

I smiled at his baby name for me. He had always called me that, just like my little cousins.

Rahul escorted me to the Colonel's reading room. He was sitting in his favourite chair by the window and I realised he would have seen me in the garden.

'Assalamu Alaikum, Uncle-ji,' I said when he looked up from his book.

'Wa Alaikum Assalam, Aster. Come in.'

'Has she been naughty?' Rahul asked hopefully.

The Colonel smiled at him. 'Quite the contrary. Have you been nice to the peacocks today?'

'Certainly, Nana-ji.' He turned to me. 'Haven't I, Asti?'

I nodded at him as he climbed onto the Colonel's knee. The Colonel still held himself like a soldier. He spent much of his time in this room reading books in many languages.

'Aster, I hear you have won a place in the Government Girls High School,' he said, his gaze appraising.

'Ji.' I ducked my head in embarrassment.

'It is a step in the right direction for your family. Girls should be educated as far as possible. Educate a girl like you and you educate a whole village.'

I looked up at him – what an interesting thing to say.

'Are you enjoying it?'

I hesitated. He wouldn't be fooled if I lied.

'Most of the subjects are easy,' I offered.

He regarded me before speaking again and I shifted my feet nervously. 'If you need extra tuition in any of them, come to me. But I suggest you knuckle down and work hard. Nothing worthwhile is achieved without pain – hmm?'

'I will. Thank you, Uncle-ji.'

How could he have guessed it was difficult for me? It was as if he knew, and here was my chance to ask his advice. Yet I didn't dare mention the attitude of the other girls or of Mrs Abdul. A man like him would shrug it off. 'Get on with it,' I could imagine him saying, and I firmly shut my mouth.

'Remember you are like a daughter to us. Any problem at all, you can confide in me.'

I nodded again. 'Shukriya.'

'Now, go and see if you can tire out this little devil while I attend prayers at the mosque.'

Rahul grinned at him and held up his hand for a high five. Then he ran out of the room in front of me. The Colonel was very kind but I doubted he could help me with Mrs Abdul. If she was reported wouldn't she hate me more?

We were passing the kitchen when the Colonel's daughter, Juli, called to me. 'Aster, wait a moment.' She had a package.

Rahul was pulling on my hand but I managed to stop.

'This is a shalwar qameez I have grown out of.' Juli patted her stomach to show how round she'd grown – she was pregnant again. 'But you may be tall enough for it now.'

'Thank you.' Her clothes always looked expensive. It would be lovely to have a new outfit for church and weddings.

'I'll leave it with your mother.' She frowned at Rahul tugging at me. 'Don't let him get away with anything, Aster. He's old enough to toe the line.'

I laughed as Rahul opened the door and burst out, pulling me behind him.

CHAPTER

7

It was Rabia's turn to be reprimanded, not by Mrs Abdul, though she watched Rabia closely, but by Miss Saed-Ulla, after she asked Rabia to read a page from *To Kill a Mockingbird*.

'Rabia, you will not pass well in your exams if you do not read the novel.'

The reprimand was gentle, unlike Mrs Abdul's, but Rabia's face paled as she hung her head.

At lunch she asked me about my maths and English. 'You can't put a foot wrong in maths class.'

I finally told her about Ijaz. 'I had a brother – older than me – there were only two of us so I wasn't as busy as my cousins with little kids to always look after. I did my homework with him and he helped me.'

Rabia stared at me. 'You sounded close. What happened?'

It took me a moment but I said it. 'He died.'

36

Her eyes watered. 'I'm sorry. I'd hate for my sister or brother to die.'

'He was always physically weak because of his lungs. My mother had to sit up with him a lot at night. Have a pot of water boiling to make steam. It meant he was often inside with his books.'

I was quiet, not sure what to say next, then remembered her question included English. 'English is my third language after Urdu. We have cousins in Australia who don't know how to write Urdu so we write in English to them. Or maybe they don't have Urdu script on their computers.' I grinned.

'Your brother also helped with English?'

I nodded.

Mrs Rafique did too; she had many English books I'd borrowed over the years, but if I told Rabia about the Rafiques then she'd know my mother was a servant. So I told her about church instead.

'But also from our fellowship – some of our religious books and songs are in English.'

I glanced at her. Now would be when I lost her interest. But what was the point of hiding who I was?

Then Rabia did something strange. She stuck her bottom lip between her teeth and shifted closer though no one was nearby. 'My father wasn't always Muslim,' she said. 'He was Masihi like you, but he couldn't get a good job. He was offered land, and money to build a house if he said the Kalimah.'

When she had finished I had no words to say; I just stared at her. Was my father capable of something like that?

'You mightn't understand,' she sat back a little, 'but he converted for us, his family. My brother is in university now. My father works in an office instead of some menial job. My sister and I will have good marriages.' Then she narrowed her gaze at me. 'You don't hate me?'

I shook my head. 'Thank you,' I managed to say. She was the first girl in the class to talk to me, let alone entrust me with her family background. I also suspected she wasn't as well accepted as it first appeared. No wonder Mrs Abdul watched her like a crane at a fishpond.

'I have an idea,' Rabia said then. 'What say you help me with English and maths and I'll help you with Arabic and Islamiyat?'

Rabia did well in Mrs Abdul's classes. 'How do you know Arabic so well?'

'We were given special classes. Plus, it's been a few years now – since the change.'

I nodded, thinking. 'Teik hai, okay. When shall we do it? Lunchtimes?'

'And after school? I don't think my father will let me go to your village. He's tried to put his old life behind him.'

I was sure Abba wouldn't mind fetching me later. Often we had to wait for Sammy.

'Teik hai, on the same days my cousin has soccer practice.' We gave each other high fives. We agreed to become Facebook friends and talk further there.

After that, Rabia helped me during breaks. Arabic was more difficult even though there were many Arabic words in Urdu. They were difficult to spell and I just had to try to remember them by rote. A dot in the wrong place could change the meaning entirely and earn a cuff over the head from Mrs Abdul.

But I was beginning to improve. Even Mrs Abdul noticed. She praised Rabia, not me, and that made other girls want to help me as well.

MESSAGES

Maryam Yusef Hey, Aster, check out my blog. It's all about what interests me – you might like it too. You can give me some ideas. There are pics from the last time we visited the land of the pure. Sorry, how insensitive of me, that was Ijaz's funeral. It's called Step by Step, just google it.

Peacock Blue Teik hai. I'll look at it. Sorry I wasn't good company when you came. It was such a shocking time.

Maryam Yusef No worries. That's Australian for everything's okay. We were so sorry about Ijaz. He was my favourite boy cousin.

Peacock Blue My favourite brother too. Khuda Hafiz, God keep you safe.

Maryam Yusef Khuda Hafiz.

Step by Step

To see a world where freedom, peace and justice reign

About Maryam Yusef Masih

I was born in Australia but my parents were born in Pakistan, the land of the pure. My mother was raised near the Azad Kashmir border and my father in a village on the outskirts of Lahore. He was very intelligent and won a scholarship to a university in London. Now he is a specialist dentist in Australia. This doesn't happen often for children born in obscure rural villages in developing countries. What would my life be like if he hadn't had that opportunity, I wonder?

Since I am Australian but Pakistani too I call myself Australian Born Pakistani, ABP. I keep in contact with my cousins in Pakistan and because I go there on holidays, I have seen the best of Pakistan – its beautiful scenery and kind hospitality. I've been to Lahore – my father says you haven't lived if you haven't been to Lahore – and to my mother's village in the north of Pakistan, in Khyber Pakhtunkhwa where some of my cousins live, and beautiful Swat. Since we look like Pakistanis and not Australians we were allowed over the border into Azad Kashmir but we couldn't see the blue lake at the top of the world because of the Line of Control and the intermittent conflict. My mother was sad about that; she hasn't seen the lake since she was young.

We go to a church in Australia – the customs are different but my parents are used to them. Men and women and children all sit together in family groups; women don't have to wear scarves and men don't wear hats inside. My brother and I don't wish for anything different.

I like Australian culture – people do as they please and don't stick to rules about how to dress, how to serve food, what to say. Many are atheists and don't feel beholden to any power more important than themselves, which can make them less respectful than they could be. But I have great friends – Anglo-Australian as well as Pakistani-Australian.

Other Australians are surprised to find we are not Muslim, and that they have more in common with us than they imagine when they first see us. Only a few patients who see Dad's face decide not to sit in his dentist's chair. We understand racial intolerance. In places like Afghanistan and Africa, ethnic cleansing is still practised just like Hitler did in World War Two. We need to stand against such abuses. Maybe I shouldn't be training as a teacher but as a lawyer. But I love learning about the world and I want kids to appreciate it and the people around them. It's the peaceful way to change the things we don't need in our world, step by step.

And one person can start.

COMMENTS

Peacock Blue Accha blog, Maryam. I haven't even been to Azad Kashmir and yet you have and you live in Australia. We have been to Swat though – that is a bahut beautiful place, with rivers, mountains, wildflowers and green meadows you can play in.

Amir It sounds like a very beautiful place, wish I could see it. Pakistan is a newly formed nation but it is an ancient land with a rich history. I am an exile but I enjoy my life in Canada too. It also is a beautiful country. According to your code, Maryam, I am a CBP.

Fatima I was born in London but I know what you mean about second-generation exile. I miss the deserts of my parents' homeland too. I am a BBA.

CHAPTER

8

I couldn't wait for Friday morning school to be over. I just had to get through Mrs Abdul's classes. Dr Amal was coming to our village to give a talk about hygiene and to inoculate the kids. He called it a medical camp. A few relatives were coming from villages further south. Barakat told Sammy on Facebook he was travelling up with his family. I never contacted Ijaz's friends on Facebook but I could see what they were doing on the newsfeed.

Saleema and her friends approached me as I came through the gate into school, and walked with me past the office. She apologised for her recent behaviour and wanted to see my homework. I'd been taught to give people second chances, yet still I hesitated, even though other girls had also offered to help.

'Just so I can see you're being advised properly.'

Saleema was the most intelligent girl in the class and the others all tipped their heads, their eyes wide and helpful.

I pulled my homework book from my backpack. Saleema pored over the pages and made marks with her pencil.

She shook her head. 'This paragraph in particular needs to be changed. You'll just have time if you do it now.' She handed the book back to me. 'It takes a long time to learn Arabic well, but you'll get it in the end.'

I sat on a bench and rewrote the section according to her pencil marks. I would show Rabia so we both could improve. But Rabia wasn't in class that day. Mrs Abdul swept in and demanded our homework. She checked it while we copied verses into our exercise books.

'Aster Suleiman!' Mrs Abdul's voice was so harsh I dropped my pen. 'Come to the front immediately.' She pointed at my new addition. 'This is unacceptable. Are you slipping again?'

I glanced at Saleema, but she shrugged her shoulders to show she didn't understand what happened. She even looked puzzled. How could *she* have got it wrong? The answer came to me as I faced Mrs Abdul: I was crazy to trust Saleema.

'I'm sorry, miss.'

I pointed to the paragraph I'd crossed out. 'Is that one correct?'

'Ji, stupid girl, but if you knew what you were doing you wouldn't have second thoughts. You must try harder. It would be easier for you if you were Muslim, then you would have enthusiasm for the subject.'

This time she smacked me with the book. It felt as if a tennis ball that Sammy had hit for six just landed on my face. I clutched my stinging cheek on the way to my desk. I knew I'd have a bruise.

When Abba collected me he didn't see my cheek; he was facing the front with the motor running. 'We'll pick up your ammi on the way,' was all he said.

There would be many preparations before Dr Amal came. We reached the Rafiques' house and I jumped out to get Ammi, but it was the Colonel who met me at the door. He must have been on his way to the garden.

'Aster?' His finger touched my cheek. 'What is this?'

I shrugged, unsure of what to say, or how much trouble I'd be in if I said anything at all.

'Did a student do this?'

I shook my head.

'A teacher?'

I stared at him miserably. What could I say?

His mouth tightened. 'Which one?'

It wasn't even a question. It was a command and I could imagine how easily he would have controlled an army of men.

'The Arabic and Islamiyat teacher.'

He frowned, but he didn't say one word against Mrs Abdul. 'Didn't I tell you to ask me if you needed help?'

I nodded. 'A student has been helping me.'

'She obviously hasn't helped enough.' How could I explain about Saleema? 'You will come here every Thursday after school and I will help you with your study.'

My heart sank. It was very kind but I had little leisure

time. His face softened. 'Just for an hour, then you can return home with your mother.'

'Thank you, you are very gracious.'

I hoped he wouldn't tell the principal, but I didn't want to make more of it by pleading with him. Ammi was ready then and we walked to the rickshaw.

'What happened to your face?'

There was no sport to blame it on, no children's games or cricket balls. 'The Arabic teacher didn't like my home-work.'

It still stung that I'd had it right. It was Saleema's fault but Mrs Abdul was right about one thing: if I really knew what I was doing I would have known Saleema was tricking me.

Ammi clucked her tongue, but whether it was at the teacher or me I couldn't tell. 'I heard the Colonel saying he'd tutor you. That's very good of him.'

The village was an ants' nest. People were arriving and villagers like us were laying out extra mattresses for guests in our second rooms. Uncle Ibrahim, Sammy and other men were cooking curries and rice in degs, huge steel pots outside the church. Barakat had found Sammy. His family had just arrived by bus and walked in from the main road. His sisters and Aunty Assia would stay with us. Sammy saw me and waved me over.

'Here's Aster.'

I had an armful of trays for the rice.

'This is Barakat,' he said unnecessarily. I knew who he was and I gave Sammy a fierce stare. I didn't want to talk to Barakat. What if I got to like him and my parents chose someone else? Besides, there would be no early marriage for me now. Abba was intent on my education.

'Salaam,' said Barakat. I returned the greeting. It was the first time we had spoken since the flood. He stared at my cheek a moment but didn't ask about my bruise. 'I see you have taken over Ijaz's wall.'

My face felt hot. So he knew it was me. What did I expect? Everyone on Ijaz's friend list must know. 'I'll make my own soon,' I mumbled.

Then he smiled. He looked so like Ijaz my mouth gaped. Sammy trod on my toe and I managed a quick smile back.

'It's good to see Ijaz's wall alive again—' Barakat stopped suddenly at his unfortunate use of words, but they didn't hurt like they would have six months ago.

'That's what I thought when I did it.'

Later, after everyone had pushed and shoved to reach the trestle tables of food and shovelled curry and rice from their plates into their mouths, they crowded into the church. Sammy played the tabla and I sang songs to lead everyone.

Then Dr Amal told us where to dig our latrines so we wouldn't get diseases, to understand water care, to boil water for babies and small children. At the end Dr Amal sang. We didn't let him stop; after 'Umeed', we begged for more.

It was late before I took Barakat's ammi and sisters home to sleep. Aunty Assia didn't speak much; she seemed tired, but Barakat's sisters told me about their trip on the bus, how a fight broke out when the conductor found a man hadn't paid and the bus stopped to throw him off.

'It was because he was Shia,' Afia said quietly. Afia was fourteen like me, but Rubina was younger and couldn't stop exclaiming about all the things she had seen.

'Dr Amal is so handsome,' she said. 'I hope I marry someone as fair.'

'He'll be rich one day too. Doctors always are.' Afia winked at me. 'And he's not even married.'

That wound Rubina up again. 'Maybe he'd notice me and ask for me. That can happen.'

'In your dreams.' Afia yawned.

'Why don't you marry Barakat?' Rubina said to me. 'Then we'd all be sisters.'

'But you'd marry someone from another village – you'd hardly ever be home,' I said.

Rubina pouted. 'You'd get married before me. We'd have a few years together.'

I thought maybe she would be married before me. She had stared at me in surprise when she heard I attended high school.

'Anyway, Barakat likes you,' Rubina added.

'Shh.' Afia cuffed her over the ear. 'That's for Ummie and Abu to decide, not you.'

'Ow.' Rubina called for her mother but she was already asleep with Ammi and Dadi-ji, my grandmother. Abba had gone to Sammy's house to sleep, with 'so many women' in ours. Rubina didn't stop chattering until I turned off the light.

I woke early before my cousins and wrote a message to Maryam on Facebook.

MESSAGES
Peacock Blue Salaam, cousin-ji. We're having a medical camp in the village – Dr Amal is giving the talks in an easy style so everyone can understand. He sang again last night. Have you seen the video clips on his Facebook page? Uncle Yunis and Aunty Assia are here with Barakat, Afia and Rubina. Hope you are all well, please give my love to your family.

Afia woke and stared over my shoulder.

'Do you want your own profile so Ijaz's friends won't see what you post?'

I could imagine her and Barakat discussing it, and I nodded. It was time.

She helped me set it up. We glanced at each other before we deactivated Ijaz's account. I thought it would be harder, that I'd feel like I did when his coffin slipped into the ground, but I didn't at all. Dadi-ji was right: Ijaz would always be with me.

Suddenly Rubina was awake, making the house sound like a dozen girls chattering, and the day clutched me by the scruff and dragged me through it. The inoculations for

49

the kids were first. When Rubina had to have hers she cried while she waited.

Aunty Assia scolded her, 'What a terrible example for the little kids, you'll make them scream. Now kharmosh, shut up.'

She did, but I think it was more to do with seeing Dr Amal appear behind the table with all the medical supplies.

'She's a silly girl,' Afia said. 'She doesn't think it will hurt if he gives it.'

Then there was more curry and naan and a special service before the visitors left the next morning. Dr Amal had to leave but we discovered something interesting we didn't know before: Barakat could sing. Sammy played the tabla for him and Afia said I should play one too. It was the most fun I'd had since Ijaz was alive.

It was another long evening telling stories to Rubina before I turned off the light. It worked like magic – as soon as the room darkened Rubina fell quiet like a little bird in a tree.

'Why is she so quiet?' I whispered to Afia.

'We don't have electric light. We blow out the lamp. In the kitchen we have a kerosene one. I think when you turn off the light here it strikes her dumb. Don't try to understand, just enjoy.'

CHAPTER

9

The cousins were leaving on Sunday morning just as I had to go to school. Abba was busy taking people to the bus adda in town, but he managed to drop me off at school first. I was late and tiptoed into the classroom. Miss Saed-Ulla was reading. Imagine if it was one of Mrs Abdul's classes – she would have made me write a hundred lines about why I mustn't be late. In Arabic!

Rabia and I ate lunch together as usual, helping each other with our work, and I told her what Saleema did.

'She knew I'd be away. Never trust her. She's mean to me as well. It's possible she knows about my family and many don't trust converts.'

I was quiet. Christians could also be like this. When an ex-Muslim visited our village some people were wary, wondering if he had recanted and was looking to accuse us.

'Anyway,' Rabia said. 'We are fortunate to be studying in this school.'

'What makes you say that?'

'The Taliban are bombing girls' schools in Swat. That's not so far away.'

'It couldn't happen here, could it, in this army town?'

'I shouldn't think so.'

I thought of the Colonel. Even if he was retired I couldn't imagine him standing by while militants bombed schools. Yet so many people in Swat were fleeing their beautiful place. When we visited there years ago, it was paradise.

Mrs Abdul still didn't let up on me – if anything she became worse – but I was learning how to survive her lessons without too many blows. If I kept my head down and did my best, my reward was not to be beaten.

This time she couldn't fault my homework. She looked disappointed and didn't praise me. 'Maybe you'll become a true Muslim yet, girl. Your study will be easier then.'

Rabia had another go at me after school. 'Why not say the Kalimah? It doesn't mean anything.'

'Are you Muslim, Rabia?'

She looked flummoxed. 'Well, in name, I suppose.'

'But do you believe that Muhammad is the last Prophet?'

She looked behind her before she answered. 'Well, not really.'

'What do you believe?'

She shrugged and when she looked at me, her eyes were miserable. 'I know there's a god. Mrs Abdul is so strict about not believing anything other than Islam, or we won't go to paradise.'

'The Injeel, the New Testament, says the same. Belief in Yesu Masih is the only thing that pleases Khuda.'

'You should convert,' Rabia said. 'It's a Muslim country, everything is easier if you're the same.'

I knew then religion was just culture to her; whichever suited her best was what she'd say she believed. How many said they believed because it was expected, because they were born here?

'It's not who I am,' I murmured but she didn't hear me.

Ammi had news for me when I returned home. In her hand she held a letter.

'What's happening?' I asked.

'Hadassah is returning to the village.'

'Wah. That's wonderful. We'll be able to do things together again. Will she come to school with me?' I was so full of questions I didn't at first notice how quiet my mother was.

'Ammi? Is everything all right?'

I thought then of the way Aunty Feebi didn't tell me where Hadassah went. How I couldn't write her an email even, and she wasn't on Facebook anymore. It was like she had disappeared from the face of the earth.

She looked at the letter and inclined her head.

'I think so.' She glanced at me. 'It's just that she won't be here for long. When she returns she will marry.'

'Marry? But she's only two years older than me!'

'It's best for her. Uncle Bashir and Aunty Feebi have found a kind and suitable man.'

I looked at her dubiously. 'Does she want to get married?'

'I'm sure she does. It's a good opportunity for her.' Ammi smiled at me. 'A wedding is good for the village.'

I thought of the mehndi party, dancing, painting patterns on our hands with henna. The ceremony in the church when the bride sometimes wore white like brides in western countries; then the walima, the wedding feast, at the groom's house when the bride would wear the traditional red tunic and long skirt.

'Hadassah and I can go shopping.' I thought of Rabia. 'My friend from school can come too.'

'I hope so,' was all Ammi said.

A few days later Hadassah arrived with her parents. Abba fetched them from the bus adda in town. When I visited them in the evening, Hadassah was different. She was older than when I saw her last, but a year shouldn't have made her seem like a woman who knew secrets that I wasn't yet privy to. Maybe that was what a marriage proposal did to a girl.

MESSAGES

Maryam Yusef Thanks for the message, Aster. The medical camp sounds a good idea. Nice to see all the cousins?

Peacock Blue Ji. Write more posts on your blog. It's good.

Maryam Yusef You could do a blog too.

Peacock Blue My English isn't good, and what would I write about? Village life in Pakistan? Who would be interested?

Maryam Yusef You'd be surprised. People are interested in other cultures and human rights. The way they treat asylum seekers and refugees at government level here is pretty appalling, but no one who thinks about moral ethics agrees.

Peacock Blue Even girls in my high school aren't interested in villages and they live here.

Maryam Yusef Australians are concerned – they get upset if a girl is bullied because she's wearing a scarf.

Peacock Blue Why would anyone bully a girl about a scarf?

Maryam Yusef Some Anglo guys picked on my friend and me on our way home, called us dirty wogs. Then one pulled my friend's scarf off. My brother had to get it back.

Peacock Blue That's shameful.

Maryam Yusef Some Australians have never travelled and they're frightened of people different from themselves. They think if people like us are let into Australia, extremists will follow.

Peacock Blue People here don't like groups like the Taliban either. But what can we do? If people don't support them they retaliate. They're bombing girls' schools in Swat now. A girl wrote a blog about it under an assumed name, Gul Makai.

Maryam Yusef Bet they know educating girls will change the world. I'm proud of you for going to high school.

Peacock Blue Guess who has returned to the village after so long?

Maryam Yusef Hadassah?

Peacock Blue Ji, she's going to be married.

Maryam Yusef That may be a blessing. Let's pray she'll be happy.

Step by Step
To see a world where freedom, peace and justice reign

Exile

A comment on my blog instigated this question: what is exile? My mother remembers the Hindu Kush – playing in the snow in January on holidays in the Murree Hills or in Azad Kashmir. She remembers mangoes so plentiful she could buy a dozen for a few rupees. When she was tiny her mother stripped her and sat her in a little tin tub to eat them. Mango juice stains a pretty outfit.

She remembers the smell of spices down the streets, the kite festivals, dancing at mehndi parties before weddings, the Kaghan streams where Sprite bottles were kept cool in canals and fishermen caught rainbow trout.

She wept when the earthquake destroyed her childhood dreams. Then came the floods. 'What can we do?' she cried. My father sent money for our families to rebuild. He went to help with constructing houses even though he only knows how to rebuild people's jaws.

My memories of mountains and an ancient Moghul landscape are secondhand. I look out at hills that are tiny in comparison but they are my hills. I love going for drives through them and visiting European-style villages and markets. I haven't played in snow but I love the beach – a place about which my mother has no memory at all. Often I wonder how my cousins fare in their rural villages as I stand in an orderly line and travel to university on an air-conditioned bus that has empty seats.

COMMENTS

Khalid I know what you mean. I live in a country that has everything – freedom of speech (as far as it can be), just laws, education, medical help, nice houses and effluent drains, cars for everyone, and most people have jobs and houses to live in. If they don't the government helps them. So many people in my extended family live in squalor in the old country my parents were born in. They don't even have a proper stove. It drives me crazy sometimes thinking, why me? Why do I have the heavenly life when so many suffer? I wish I could help more.

Maryam Yeah, whenever I go back to my roots I enjoy seeing my grandmother and cousins, and the place is beautiful, but it's not long before I feel this guilt that I've been singled out. I don't think it's wrong to be rich, but I've been brought up to believe that resources are given to share. My father always sends money to make sure there is education for both boys and girls in the village he came from. But we get upset when we hear of anyone being exploited – usually those who have no money or power to do anything about it.

Shafique Like survivor guilt. I've felt it too. When I was a teen I didn't like going back, I got picked on for having money in my pocket and the beggars drove me crazy.

No one thought I could understand their life. But now I'm in uni I can see things a bit clearer. People want respect whatever situation they are in. Nor do they always want a handout. I can think of things to do now that don't offend so much.

Sabha I cannot return to where my parents were born as it is too dangerous, but my mother misses the beauty of it before the war started. It is hard for me to imagine. They have no photos.

CHAPTER

10

Once started the wedding machine can't be stopped. Once you're strapped in there's no hope of disentanglement.

So much to plan: food, the ceremony, music, clothes, and not just for the bride and groom. And the pace heightens the closer the wedding looms, like a barrel rolling down a steep hill.

Everyone, young and old, talks about the food. Guests judge the success of a wedding by the dishes chosen and how much is laid out on the long tables. Is there chicken masalah and sweet coloured rice? Is the naan hot? In our village, food for weddings was still cooked the old way, in degs, by the barber and any man he could rope in to help stir the huge steel pots.

Many of the wedding customs were developed before Islam or Christianity came to this country, and we follow them, adding our Christian customs to the mix.

One of my jobs was keeping the younger cousins out of everyone's way. They always wanted stories and songs, so I helped look after Sammy's brother and sisters, Akeel, Marya and Noori, while Aunty Rakel sewed. I picked up Sammy's tabla and beat out a rhythm for us to sing until they ran off to play.

Amid the flurry I finally managed to talk to Hadassah alone. It had been difficult as she didn't go to the well anymore, or visit us. I hadn't even seen her at the village shop. But I caught her at home after school when her mother went with Ammi to a cloth shop in town. I wondered at first why she hadn't gone with them.

'I missed you.' I sat on the charpai, the string bed beside her.

I was surprised at how little she spoke. She used to be so full of life and I thought more seriously about what had happened to her. It still obviously affected her.

'Did I ever say how sorry I was that day when . . . when it happened?'

Her eyelids flew up and she looked directly at me. 'It could not have been avoided – they were lying in wait. If it wasn't me, it would have been you.'

I frowned. I hadn't thought of it like that. And that was the moment when I finally did my arithmetic. I wasn't a little child anymore. She wouldn't just have been beaten – there was blood on her shalwar – and suddenly I understood it all.

'I'm really sorry, I didn't understand—' I paused. 'But the wedding is good, isn't it?'

Hadassah still hadn't smiled. 'It's what I must do, to make a life for myself. Maybe I'll have other children.'

The room spun around me and stopped so suddenly I thought I'd slip off the charpai. There was so much I hadn't been told – probably to save her honour and that of her family as much as to protect my innocence.

A year away – of course – why hadn't I thought of it before?

'So you never knew?' She sighed as I shook my head.

We were quiet awhile until I asked, 'Did you enjoy the tailoring course?'

She nodded mechanically. 'It's what I always wanted to do. I can even make my own patterns. And when I graduated with a diploma, I got a sewing machine of my own.' She spoke as if she was reciting her times tables and pointed to the corner. The machine was still in its case.

'Nay, I don't feel like marrying,' she said then as if I had just asked. 'But Ammi says it is the best thing.'

I stared at her as a tear rolled down her cheek.

'They made me give him away. No one would have married me with a child.'

There were no words I could say. Abba always said when we're tested by fire our faith would be refined, but what did I know of suffering? Nothing compared with Hadassah's pain.

I took her hand. 'How can I help?'

'Pray for me. I never knew how hard it would be, but I had to do it for his sake. No one but my family would believe I was forced. And in this country it doesn't matter which religion you are – in an instance like this, the girl is at fault, she has broken the law.'

Her words were hollow and dark, like her eyes.

'Can I come with you to shop for the wedding? Will that help a little?'

She tilted her head.

'We'll go to the bazaar tomorrow after school?'

It would be difficult for her, I knew, but she looked bravely at me. If only I could cheer her up, help her be the bright and bubbly girl she had been.

'Does your fiancée know about the baby?'

A tiny shake. 'I shouldn't think so. He is older. His wife died recently and he needs a mother for his children.'

'You'll be good at that.'

'I don't feel like it. Not yet. But my parents want me married before rumours start or anything else happens.'

'That can't be true.' Was she joking? I held my breath at this glimmer of levity.

She gave a small smile. 'This opportunity came up. Not many girls' families would take it.' Then she added, 'Would they have offered if they knew?'

I was silent, wondering if Hadassah would ever tell him.

Rabia came to the bazaar with us. She chattered away – one of the reasons I'd asked her along, as I couldn't bring myself to talk about mundane things after what Hadassah had just told me. Our task was to buy cloth and bangles for the younger cousins' new outfits, and to get dupattas dyed to match.

We visited the new emporium first. Everything was too expensive but it was lovely fingering the silks. I was glad I didn't have to worry about a new outfit; I had Juli Rafique's shalwar qameez to wear. We ventured down to the usual bazaar, covering our heads when we heard the azan, the call to prayer.

At cloth shop after cloth shop the men spread out samples for us to view. One young man threw cloth in the air so it would settle right in front of us like silk birds, colour after flying colour. He'd guessed one of us was a bride when Rabia picked up a red wedding dupatta. We liked his cloth the best, and bought ten pieces along with enough gauzy material for the dupattas.

He held up a red wedding outfit. 'Very beautiful.'

His gaze brushed us all; he hadn't decided who was the bride.

Hadassah made an effort but Rabia noticed her reticence. 'You are a perfect bride, Hadassah, not wanting to leave your family.'

A quick flush of annoyance spread across Hadassah's face but Rabia obviously thought it was a blush.

'How exciting this all is for you. I won't be able to get married for years yet.' She held the red wedding dupatta over Hadassah's head and the gold fringe framed her face.

'Ji, this is suiting you too much.' The young man tipped his head from side to side in happiness.

Hadassah's eyes were startled as if she were a gazelle, unsure which way to run to escape the hunter.

Reaching up I gently removed the dupatta. 'Aunty Feebi and Ammi will come with Hadassah to buy her clothes.'

'And the groom's too?' Rabia asked.

'Ji.' I stuffed the cloth into two bags and handed one to Hadassah.

'Is he tall, handsome? Rich?' That was Rabia.

It was then I wondered at the sense of inviting her and changed the subject.

'How is your English study, Rabia? Are you practising with your sister, reading to her?'

Rabia made a face. 'She laughs at me, and my brother says why bother as I'll get married anyway. What will I need English for then?'

'To teach your children.' This came from Hadassah, the first thing she'd said all day other than a greeting, forced out of her by politeness.

Rabia and I stared at her.

'Mothers are the best teachers. That's why girls need to go to school.' Hadassah's voice sounded choked, as if she would cry, and I jumped in with a comment of my own.

'I think it would be good to work after marriage anyway. Why do we have to stop? Hadassah, you will work once you're married, won't you?' I couldn't imagine her not sewing.

Hadassah looked at me blankly. 'You'll sew clothes when you're married?' I prompted.

'Ji, I believe that was mentioned,' but her voice was flat again.

Rabia was gazing at Hadassah with interest and, too late, I realised I'd led the conversation down the marriage path again.

'What about your study for your exams, Rabia?' I moved to another stall so they would follow me.

'I should be fine.' Then she had her revenge on me. 'Are you practising your Arabic and verses? You have to pass that to reach the next level.'

'I'm trying my best.'

I thought of the Colonel. The first tutoring session was easier than lessons at school. If only he could come to school to teach us all Arabic, we'd be proficient in no time.

We pored over the rows and rows of circles in the bangle shop. Hadassah's parents would buy her gold ones if they could afford it, but we bought glass ones for the children, sets of two dozen to match each piece of cloth. Shoes would have to wait until their mothers could bring them to the bazaar.

Down by the river the dyer pinned swatches of cloth to each piece of dupatta. 'Three days,' he said.

Rabia gave us chai and biscuits after we walked to her house while I rang Abba to collect Hadassah and me. We squeezed into the back of the rickshaw and were quiet on the way to the village.

Hadassah had appeared tired and listless, and now I understood why. It was her excessive sadness. My mind turned to Rabia's words about exams. What if I didn't do well enough to continue? What if Abba decided my education wasn't worth the money spent?

I knew then, regardless of Islamiyat and Arabic, I wanted very much to study, to be a teacher and an independent woman. Like Maryam.

MESSAGES

Peacock Blue Salaam, Afia. Are you coming to the wedding?

Afia Yunis Ji, just received invitation. Bahut pretty.

Peacock Blue Accha. Did you know our cousin Maryam in Australia has a blog? If you have any ideas for her to write about she will be happy.

Afia Yunis Wah, it will be good to practise my English. It's not in Urdu?

Peacock Blue Nay, she's proper Australian. She calls herself Aussie. The website's called Step by Step. You can google it.

Afia Yunis Teik hai, I'll look at it.

Peacock Blue Say salaam to Aunty Assia and Uncle Yunis and all your family.

Step by Step

To see a world where freedom,
peace and justice reign

Changing the World One Girl at a Time

I heard from my cousin that girls' schools are being destroyed in the mountains of Pakistan but I haven't seen it on our news. Our news is full of reports that presumably relate to us – the new boy on next season's football team, political arguments that everyone is sick of, which schools have the best reading scores, maybe a terrorist attack in Syria – but no news of little schools in an unknown part of the Himalayas.

I believe our neighbours don't just live next door. If you think of the earth as part of a huge universe, then all people on earth are our neighbours. Imagine your local school being bombed. Okay, some get graffitied or burned over summer when delinquents get bored, but imagine if it was destroyed because there were girls studying in it. We Australians wouldn't stand for that. Those girls in Swat are our neighbours – they live on this planet with us. So what can we do?

I have found a blog of such a girl who urges the world to not turn away. She believes girls deserve an education too. Her school was destroyed but she is not giving up – she is studying at home and writing a blog. But she doesn't give her real name. She calls herself Gul Makai, Cornflower, the heroine of many Pakhtun folktales.

COMMENTS

Amir A society is healthy if all people have equal rights to education, freedom and services.

Peacock Blue I am the first girl in my village to go to high school and I am thankful for the opportunity. Girls need to be educated to pass knowledge to their children.

Tamsin What about the 280 Nigerian girls who can't have an education now? Boko Haram militants don't care about girls' education.

Shafique Isn't that more to do with war and gaining a territory?

Habib It makes too much change in poor countries if girls get educated like boys.

Fozia Don't we want that change?

Habib What if culture is damaged?

Fozia What are you worried about? I know many educated women who still follow their culture and faith.

Abdulla Girls should not be educated. They are not as intelligent as boys and will become proud, make wrong decisions, and be difficult to handle. Those Nigerian girls will be better off away from their kafir parents.

Fozia I'm not going to comment on the lack of intelligence of your views, Abdulla – shame.

CHAPTER

11

Rabia and I continued to help each other with our home-work and I studied with the Colonel on Thursday afternoons. My primary school teacher, Miss Saima, visited to find out how my studies were going – she even checked my English essay on *To Kill a Mockingbird*. I wrote about racism and how we mustn't fear or disregard those different from ourselves. I must admit I had a vested interest, being the unpopular girl in class, but this had been happening since the beginning of time. Cain killed Abel because Abel was different and received more favour than him. How much bullying of others is born of fear and the desire for power? I was glad Mrs Abdul would not be reading my English essay.

'Learn it by heart,' Miss Saima advised. 'It is a good essay.'

Learning by rote is what we always do – it was how I was going to pass the Arabic and Islamiyat exams. I could imagine Miss Rehmat saying, 'No need to learn by heart if you understand what you are doing.'

Mrs Abdul believed Arabic would miraculously become clear to me as soon as I became Muslim, that I would have an 'open window' into a new way of thinking. It was her constant hope.

It was difficult to study when Aunty Feebi was in the house in the evening to discuss wedding menus with Ammi, and clothes designs with Abba. He was sewing everyone's new clothes. Other men who could sew were commissioned to help. If Ijaz were alive he would be sewing too.

Hadassah offered to help with the children's clothes but they only let her do a few.

I hadn't managed to tempt Hadassah to the bazaar again. Soon she wouldn't be able to leave the house even if she wanted to. A week before the wedding she'd have to wear old clothes and stay inside as a symbol of moving from an old life to the new. But these days staying at home wasn't difficult for Hadassah.

Time was running out if I wanted to help her recover. Even Ammi said to Abba they should have waited a year – then Hadassah could have enjoyed her wedding.

I visited Hadassah every day after school during her lonely week. On the last day I brought nail polish and gave her a massage and a pedicure. When I turned to leave Hadassah grabbed my hand.

'Aster, can you stay longer?'

'Zarur, certainly.'

'I just want to thank you for all you've done for me.'

'This is what we do at weddings.'

'Nay, not just that. The way you care.'

If only I could do more. 'It's only a little.'

'I appreciate it. It's just that I can't stop thinking about the baby. They let me name him. I called him Shahbaz.'

I felt a prickle at the back of my eyes. Many Christian babies were called Shahbaz after the minister for minorities, Shahbaz Bhatti, but it was also the name of our great-grandfather, the first person of our family to convert from Hinduism to Christianity during the Raj. This country was India then. Even Maryam in Australia shares our great-grandfather.

'That's a beautiful thing to do, Hadassah. Maybe you'll see him one day, when he's grown. You'll see a young man walking down the bazaar who looks like your father—'

'And I'll always wonder if that is him.' She burst into sobs. 'I'll never see him again. The couple adopting him are from Australia, but I was told they'd keep his name.'

I sat on the charpai beside her and held her until she stopped shaking. After she blew her nose, she said, 'The nurse told me the couple had waited seven years for a baby. The husband grew up here. They were so happy to have Shahbaz.'

I thought at least she knew where he was, and that he was well looked after. 'We'll be able to pray for him every day. You'll still be his birth mother.'

Strangely, Hadassah smiled. 'Ammi said I needed to cry. I couldn't – it had to be such a secret that I shut myself up to keep the secret safe.' Then she said, 'That couple saved my life.'

I frowned at her.

'You know what could happen if anyone in town heard I had a child alone? I'd be jailed for being with a man who wasn't my husband. I'd be accused of zina.'

Zina. Even rape came under the category of zina if you couldn't find four male witnesses. It wasn't fair, but that was the way things were.

'It's been good to tell you.'

I gave her a squeeze. 'You are my big sister. I can come to stay with you in the holidays.'

Her eyes brightened, and I saw a glimmer of the old Hadassah.

'You are strong, Hadassah. Abba says Khuda doesn't give us a journey so hard we can't walk it with him.'

She squeezed me back. 'I have a path that is much too difficult for me, but thank you. I'll try to remember I don't walk it alone.'

I went into Sammy's house to mind his little brother and sisters while their mother sewed their clothes. Aunty Rakel sat cross-legged in front of the machine on the floor inside. Akeel, Marya and Noori were bickering in the courtyard while Sammy finished his lunch.

'Asti, tell us a story,' ten-year-old Noori said as soon as she saw me. 'A wedding one.'

'Ji, ji.'

Little Marya climbed into my lap before I'd even settled on a cushion. Akeel wasn't so sure, but I started my favourite story.

'Once there was a Persian king who ruled all the land from India to Africa. His wife had annoyed him by not coming to an important banquet and so the court decided to choose a new queen. The most beautiful girls in the kingdom were brought to the palace harem by their fathers and spent a year learning how to act like a princess.'

'Are we beautiful?' Marya asked. 'Hadassah's using whitening cream to make her skin fairer for the photographs. All the Bollywood actresses and girls on TV are fairer than us.'

She was right: every ad had a fair-skinned girl with her brown hair fanning out from her face and light eyes, her dupatta flying to heaven. We all had black hair and dark eyes.

'That doesn't mean we're not beautiful,' Noori said quickly.

'I think you're all beautiful.' Sammy said it easily like he always said things, but he didn't laugh, and when I looked up he was staring at me. It was the first time he made me feel uncomfortable.

'See?' Noori said to Marya. 'Darker skin is beautiful too. It's the way Khuda made us.'

Sammy tilted his head at me and suddenly, talk of beauty didn't seem appropriate – he and I weren't little children anymore.

'Don't you have to help the men put up the shamiana for the wedding?' I asked. The marquee was huge; they would need all the help they could get.

He left with a grin.

'Now, where were we?'

'In the harem,' Akeel said.

I stared at him in surprise – so, he had been listening.

'Accha, there was a girl called Hadassah. Her guardian and cousin, Mordecai, called her by a Persian name, Aster, and brought her to the harem to be considered as the new queen. She was not only beautiful but she was also kind and all loved her, especially the chief eunuch who looked after the harem. She grew even more beautiful with the special treatment, but there was one thing she hadn't told—'

'She was a Jew,' Marya said.

'Ji, but when the king met Aster he liked her best.'

'How did he know?' Akeel asked.

'It's called love at first sight,' Noori said.

'Will Hadassah have love at first sight tomorrow?' Marya asked.

'She might.' I hoped her groom would.

'Actually the king was so happy with Aster, he put a crown on her head and made her his new queen. They had a huge banquet, a party—'

'Like Hadassah's tomorrow?' Noori asked.

'Ji, just like our wedding feast. They even had a public holiday all through the kingdom and the king gave gifts.'

'What sort of gifts?' Akeel said.

'Probably money and letting prisoners out of jail.'

'Hadassah will get money when she's married too. We've already bought a money necklace,' Marya said. 'And I'm allowed to put it on her.'

At that all three of them ran off.

'I'm the bride!' Noori said.

'No, I am!' Marya called after her.

'I'll be the groom.' That was Akeel, and no one argued.

Relatives began arriving in hordes. Our village was like a rickshaw adda. Afia and Barakat's family were the first. Then Uncle Yusef, Aunty Noori and Maryam arrived in a proper taxi. They had managed to get a flight from Australia in time.

Maryam hugged me tight. 'How are you now?'

She was just like a big sister. 'So much better now you're here. Tonight's the mehndi night – it will be fun.'

I took her into our house. She'd have to share my charpai but she didn't complain. That night Afia, Maryam and I, with all the girl cousins and aunts, danced and sang in Hadassah's house. I played the tabla and we sang old wedding songs and Masihi praise ones like 'Jai Jai Jai'.

No one remarked on Hadassah's quietness – that was how a bride was meant to be. We were all dying to see the groom. Hadassah wouldn't tell us anything about him, which was demure, but I did wonder if she had met him yet.

I awoke the next morning to the smell of spices cooking. Maryam was still asleep from what she called jetlag. Onions and meat were being poured into the degs when I emerged outside. Hadassah would be getting dressed in her white long gown that one of the aunties brought from Lahore; Aunty Assia would be doing her hair and make-up. A few hours later the rest of us assembled in the church, men on one side and ladies on the other. We women and girls all wore dupattas on our heads in church; even Maryam covered her hair although she was western.

Hadassah was two hours late but no one minded. I had a good chat with Maryam about uni and school. I glanced over to the right and found Barakat observing me. Sammy noticed and drew him into a whispered conversation.

The groom stepped up to stand at the front of the church with a man who must have been his brother, they looked so alike. The groom was old, even older than Dr Amal, maybe even thirty, but he didn't look ugly. He wore a cream shalwar qameez with a Nehru-collared coat and a long silk scarf.

When Uncle Bashir walked in with Hadassah in a white western veil I saw the way the groom looked at her. There was compassion in his gaze. He too had suffered recently. He promised that he would support, love and protect Hadassah. It seemed as if he knew all about her. What if he did? Only a man living by God's spirit of love could accept such a situation, and my heart swelled with hope. Maybe he was such a man.

The guests enjoyed the chicken curry and the sweet rice afterwards with its multicoloured grains.

'Hmm,' Maryam said after a mouthful. 'We don't get this often enough in Australia.'

'We only ever have it at weddings.' I watched the children fighting to reach the tables of food, but I couldn't be bothered telling them off.

Hadassah had changed into the Pakistani red bridal skirt and long tunic and sat under the colourful shamiana with the groom, who we now knew was called Danyal Peter. My family was pleased, especially Dadi-ji, as it was the name of Dada-ji, my paternal grandfather who died when I was little.

The next day we all travelled in buses to Danyal's village near Rawalpindi, where his family put on a feast for us. Weddings were not about the bride and groom, but about families joining together, and Hadassah's parents were bursting with pride. The Peters were a respected Christian family; Danyal's father was a pastor like Abba.

There was only one chance to meet with Hadassah without a mob before the four days were over. Maryam was with me and we were in Hadassah's new home in Rawalpindi, about to leave. Hadassah wore a beautiful pink shalwar qameez with shining stones like zircon embedded in the bodice. I'd never seen her look so beautiful.

'Will you be all right?' I asked for want of something better to say.

She took me seriously and tilted her head. 'I think so. He seems kind and so does his mother, which is even more important.'

Maryam and I grinned, pleased Hadassah's humour was returning.

'He's sad, but I understand that. I have met his children. There are two.' She stopped, finding it hard to speak, then swallowed and began again with a smile. 'They are young. The boy is still a toddler.'

Her eyes filled and I held her, thankful for Khuda's mercy. The boy would become hers. If Maryam wondered why Hadassah was overcome, she didn't ask. After all, brides cried a lot at weddings.

'Be happy,' I said. 'And join Facebook so I can tell you everything. Like my results from my exams next week.'

'At least you'll be able to study now the wedding is over.'

'Let me know when I can visit like a proper younger sister.'

'I'll keep in touch too,' Maryam said. 'It's been great to spend this time together.'

We all hugged, and we left Hadassah in the home she would share with Danyal, his children and parents, his three sisters and his brother's family.

MESSAGES

Peacock Blue Salaam, Maryam. You will be back in Australia by now, I think. It was wonderful seeing you again, even though it was short. Thank you so much for coming.

Maryam Yusef That's what family is for – I'm just glad we could get a flight in time.

Peacock Blue I'll put pics of the wedding on Facebook soon. So tired. Exams in a few days.

Maryam Yusef So now we have relatives in Rawalpindi too.

Peacock Blue Ji, relatives everywhere. Must sleep. Khuda Hafiz.

Maryam Yusef God bless your study.

CHAPTER
12

The exams loomed close like a monsoon, with the same heavy feeling in the air. Rabia had been to a shrine to pray for success in the exams.

'I want to be a teacher,' she said. 'I have to get good results.'

She wasn't the only one. We all had to do well, not only to satisfy the teachers but also our families. The final few days before the exams I was let off the chores. Noori fed the hens and carried water. Ammi did the washing at the canal all by herself.

'We want you to do well,' Ammi said, 'but don't get used to this treatment. After the exams you will have Noori's quota of water for a week.'

I still spent time with Dadi-ji, which was no chore at all, and took the goats to graze but I carried *To Kill a Mockingbird* with me to memorise quotes while I watched them.

The Islamiyat and Arabic exams were both on the first day and these were the ones I'd spent the most time on.

I even took to watching Islamic programs in Arabic on TV. Ammi looked worried when she caught me, but I put her fears at rest. 'The only way to be educated in this country is to know Islam, but I won't convert.'

'I wish we'd had the money to send you to the Christian Girls High School,' she said. 'But it is a boarding school deep in the mountains.'

'I wouldn't want to leave you,' I said quickly.

How lonely Abba and Ammi would be with no Ijaz and me away. She kissed my cheeks and finished preparing dinner, a chore I usually did.

In class that first exam day we were given a blank booklet. We recited prayers and I said a few of my own. Then Mrs Abdul placed a page upside-down on each of our desks. None of us moved. My eyes never left her face. She returned to the front and stared at each of us and, it seemed, especially at me.

'Start!' she snapped. It was like the start of a race. All those pages whizzed over and pens scratched on paper. Some questions were taken directly from our homework and I relaxed. I had a good memory, I would pass. I managed to complete all the answers that were required in Urdu. I approached it clinically, reminding myself that I was just repeating information for an exam. *I don't believe all this.*

Then the Arabic questions began. It was an effort getting it all finished in the two hours and near the end I panicked. A question called for a passage praising the Prophet. I tried to write the correct text from the Qur'an, but I couldn't remember exactly how to spell a word. Was the letter a baab or a taab, one dot or two? The bell to put down our pens sounded and I quickly wrote in the word.

After we handed in the papers we were allowed a break before the next exam.

I sat with Rabia in the lunch area and we went over the questions. It seemed as though I had answered most things correctly and I smiled at her in relief. She was about to speak but her gaze slipped above my shoulder and her face froze, her mouth still open. I looked behind me to see what was wrong. Mrs Abdul and a man in a navy blue shirt and khaki trousers were walking towards us.

A police officer?

It was as if all the girls in the yard became statues; only their eyes moved, watching. What could a policeman want at school?

Mrs Abdul and the officer stopped in front of me and I stood in respect. She had been angry with me constantly, regularly beat me, but she had never spat words at me like she did then, as if I was a bazaar dog with rabies.

'This is the girl, officer, who blasphemed the Holy Prophet, Peace Be Upon Him.'

Rabia gave a cry. I couldn't say a word; I was too shocked.

'There must be some mistake, she wouldn't . . .' Rabia's voice trailed away as Mrs Abdul's gaze bored into her.

'Be careful, Rabia. If you support her you could be arrested too. This malaise is catching.'

Rabia shut her mouth but I finally found my voice. 'Why is this happening? Is it the exam? I tried my best.'

Surely they couldn't arrest me for doing badly in an exam?

'Dirty kafir, you finally showed your true colours! You cursed the Holy Prophet, Peace Be Upon Him, in your paper.'

My eyes stung. 'I'm sorry, I didn't mean to. W–what did I write?'

Mrs Abdul wouldn't tell me. Was it the spelling? Should it have been two dots after all? I couldn't even remember what I dashed down at the end, but surely it wouldn't have made a blasphemous word.

The officer produced handcuffs; they were heavy and looked ancient. He pulled my hands behind my back and I felt the click of iron like a thud. None of the other girls spoke on my behalf. Their fear was as palpable as mine. Even Saleema paled. Rabia was weeping. I could still hear her as I walked with the police officer towards the outside gate.

We had just passed the office when Miss Saed-Ulla stepped in front of us. 'There must be an explanation,' she said. 'This girl is law-abiding. She would not wilfully blaspheme.'

We were too close to the gate. A mullah on his way to the mosque heard her words. By the time the principal had joined us and Mrs Abdul had finished explaining to Miss Saed-Ulla how evil I was, there was a crowd gathering on the road.

'We don't want blasphemers,' one man called out. I sensed the fear in his voice, for it echoed mine.

'Try her under Sharia law, kill her,' another said.

The officer called for reinforcements on his mobile. Within minutes there were a dozen police at the gate, pushing men away.

'We will have to take her to the station now whether we want to or not,' the first officer said to the principal. His exasperation had an edge to it. 'There will be a riot otherwise.'

Mrs Abdul spat at me through the gate. 'Now you'll have to become Muslim to save yourself.'

I wondered if I had converted right then, would she have recanted, said it was all a mistake?

One of the younger policemen bundled me into the black police van. He actually pushed me from behind with his hand, squeezing under my buttocks. I landed on the floor as he locked me in, and that was when I wept in earnest. I had never been touched like that by a man and the shock of it shamed me. I thought of my father, and my more pressing problem took over. I couldn't ring him, there had been no time to get my backpack. We always left our phones in our bags during class. The enormity of my situation began to thunder in my brain. I couldn't ring him anyway with handcuffs on.

Handcuffs? Why did they need to handcuff me? I was just a schoolgirl.

Abba would come to collect me from school in a few hours. What would they tell him? Would he be safe? Could he do anything to help me? Everyone knows that once Christians go to jail they rarely come out.

And people accused of blasphemy can be murdered before they even reach jail.

CHAPTER

13

The police van stopped outside the station. I could see the younger officer through the bars, coming to unlock the door.

'Ao, come. Jaldi, jaldi, quickly.' He gestured to me, continually glancing back the way we had come.

I stood and stepped towards him. He held out a hand as I leaned forward, then withdrew it. With my hands cuffed behind my back it was just enough to tip me off balance. I slipped, then fell to the ground. He stood there watching me struggle to my knees. I had no idea how much we need our arms to balance with.

I could hardly rise. I didn't want to ask him to help, but he reached forward and dragged me up by the cuffs. I tried not to gasp from the pain in my wrists and shoulders. The tears came unwillingly as he pushed me in the back to walk in front of him. I almost tripped again. I'd done nothing wrong; he had no right to treat me like this. But I was too frightened to speak.

Inside, there was a bench with an officer sitting behind it, typing. Another officer took me aside.

'Where are your things?'

'I don't have any.'

'No cell phone?'

I shook my head. I didn't dare look at him.

He frisked me and his hands lingered on my front. There was nothing I could do with my hands cuffed. My dupatta had fallen from my head and hung uselessly around my neck. I may as well have been naked. He checked my pocket, tickling my thigh as he did so. I tried to pull away but he grinned at me and pushed me towards a desk where an older officer sat.

I stood waiting until the officer decided to notice I was there. He made a show of finishing what he was writing. He was a big man, twice the size of Abba – he certainly didn't work in the fields. Two other officers materialised beside me.

The senior officer threw down his pen suddenly and I jumped. He leaned back in his chair and observed me.

'So, you are frightened. You should be. This is a serious charge. Blasphemy.' He said the last word slowly as he brought his hands in front of him and rested the tips of his fingers against each other like a tent.

'What did you say to insult our religion?'

'Nothing. I said nothing at all.'

The young policeman from the van coughed. 'It was an exam, sir. She wrote the blasphemy.'

'What did you expect to gain from that? Only your teacher would see it.'

'I didn't write any blasphemy. I didn't mean to,' I said.

The senior officer leaned forward. '"Didn't mean to" isn't good enough. We have to uphold the law here, and blasphemy is very serious.'

He pulled a pad of forms towards him and picked up his pen. In the quiet I could hear a commotion outside, shouts. The officer who had spoken to the principal ran with some others from back rooms to stand at the front door. They had firearms at the ready.

It took the senior officer a long time to fill out the First Investigation Report. He asked many questions that either I or one of the young officers who collected me answered. The three policemen stood to attention near me, as if I needed guarding. The senior officer left the room with the form and the man who had bundled me into the van and frisked me said, 'I know you Masihi girls go with men before you're married. I've seen how American women act in films.'

He slipped closer to me and I tried to step backwards but the wall was behind me. He shoved me so that my head hit the bricks too hard and my wrists felt as if they were being sawn through. My head spun in circles, but not one of the other men intervened even though they must have been watching. He pressed himself against me as if he was hugging me. It was nothing like my father's hugs and I screamed.

He slapped my face just as the senior officer returned. I squeezed my eyes shut to stop them filling.

'Ikram! Leave her alone,' the senior officer snapped.

'She's nothing, who cares what happens to her? We could throw her out the front door right now and that mob would tear her apart.'

The older police officer stared at the younger man until he stepped away from me, but no one apologised. The senior officer told Ikram to uncuff me. Ikram pulled me around and unlocked the cuffs. A sudden pain shot through my arms as I brought them to the front to straighten my glasses.

The senior officer asked for my signature. I was still fretting about what could have happened if he had taken longer to return. He handed me the pen and I stepped forward to scan the form, my arms throbbing. There were details about me, then I saw the words 'Accused of blasphemy, in accordance with article 295c of the Pakistani penal code'.

Was I supposed to sign this? I wished someone was there to advise me. But being accused didn't mean I did it. Surely signing wouldn't mean I'd confessed?

They all watched me. The fat one at the desk had his eyebrows raised. He glanced at the pen and I fleetingly wondered what would happen if I didn't sign.

Would they threaten me? Would I be tortured? I decided it was just an information form. I wasn't confessing to anything, just saying that the information was true.

My hand shook as I signed 'Aster Suleiman Masih'. The signature didn't look like mine but I put the pen down with as much dignity as I could manage.

'May I go home now? My parents will wonder where I am.'

The senior officer narrowed his eyes at me. 'You aren't going anywhere tonight.' He glanced at Ikram. 'Put her in the holding cell until we're told what to do with her.'

I wished the senior officer would take me himself. I didn't want to be anywhere with Ikram. I glanced back at the senior officer with what I hoped was a pleading look as Ikram led me away. Hadn't he seen with his own eyes Ikram abusing me?

The senior officer clicked his fingers and the other two officers followed us. It didn't make me feel any better. Ikram walked like a stork. When Ijaz and I were younger we'd imitate the way people walked or spoke. We found it funny, but there was nothing amusing about Ikram. One of the other officers unlocked the door. His staring unnerved me. Ikram pushed me inside and followed. I backed away – there was no one else in the cell. I could see into the next cell, where a man sat on the floor, watching us.

Ikram smirked at me as though he knew my thoughts. 'You silly girl. You will never be safe, not even in jail.'

Jail? I glanced up at him. 'I'm innocent. I'll go home as soon as they realise it was all a mistake.'

I hated the way my voice sounded, like I was asking a question, and Ikram gleefully answered, 'You'll never go home, so you had better get used to your new life.' He clapped a piece of iron with a chain hanging from it around my wrist.

'But nothing's been proved.'

'It doesn't matter with blasphemy. You hear that mob out there?'

There were still shouts and sounds like stones being thrown at the walls.

'Wouldn't you rather be in here with us?'

The youngest officer was staring at me in distaste but the other one couldn't keep his gaze off my mouth, my hair, my chest. I pulled my dupatta closer around my head and tried to cover my front. Ikram stood back but not before he had squeezed my other arm so tight I winced.

'You would be beautiful if your skin was fairer.'

He let go of my arm and ran a finger down my cheek. I turned away but his head came so close I thought he would try to kiss me. I tried to show how disrespectful I thought he was without actually looking at him – I didn't want to give him any encouragement.

I caught his grin, showing all the evil in his heart. A flash of Hadassah struggling on the ground shot through my mind. Did those boys bait her like this?

'You'll soon lose your high and mighty ways. You'll be like everyone else, trying to survive. Just let me know when you're ready to play.'

'Ikram!' The fat officer's voice boomed in the short corridor. 'Get a unit out the front and disperse that crowd. Fire over their heads. They'll be breaking windows next.'

Ikram left and the youngest man locked the door; it was just a barred gate like the one we used for our goats. 'You should be ashamed, insulting Islam. You deserve everything you're going to get.'

Was it bullying or intimidation? Whatever it was, it worked: I was miserable. I looked around the cell. There was nothing except two buckets on the cement floor. There wasn't even a partition around the buckets to hide me from the man in the next cell. How was I supposed to relieve myself? There was no charpai, so I stood, listening to the shouts and shots outside. I wiped the sweat from my neck with my dupatta. It was hot and stuffy with no fan.

Finally, I was too tired to keep standing. I sat on the cement floor with my aching arms around my legs. I rested my head on my knees, my mind blank from the shock. Never in my thoughts or worst nightmares had I ended up in jail.

I was roused by a voice I recognised. He was shouting. 'Bebekoof! You imbecile! What are you doing arresting innocent schoolgirls? Your superiors will hear about this.'

The senior officer raised his voice too. 'She has already been accused. Our hands are tied in such cases. You must understand this, Colonel Sahib.'

'I demand to see her.'

Perhaps they couldn't stop him, for there he was outside the cell. 'Aster, my god.'

I stood. The sight of him made me cry.

'Beti, you have to be brave. They won't give bail in blasphemy cases. I told them you are a child but they are not listening. I am sorry I cannot take you home.'

'I didn't do it,' I whispered.

'Of course you didn't. No one in their right mind will believe you did.' His face was flushed; his thick white eyebrows bristled together. He would look formidable to someone who didn't know him as I did.

'Why didn't Abba come?'

He glanced behind him and lowered his voice. 'I don't want to frighten you more than you must be, but there is a mob of men outside who would—' He broke off. 'I bring his love, beti. I am sorry I didn't bring anything for you – I thought they'd let me take you, considering your age.'

I gulped on a sob I tried to swallow.

His fingers clenched the bars. 'Come here, beti.'

When I reached him he slipped his hand through the bars and laid it on my head in blessing. 'May God protect you and vindicate you and keep you strong.'

Then he whispered, perhaps to himself, 'Allah, be merciful.' His eyes watered as he looked away.

I heard him as he left. 'She is just a child, and if any one of you touches her, I'll have him jailed.'

There were sniggers as he left, then everything went quiet inside except for office noises. The mob outside was still shouting. It was dark in the corridor now. I'd be able to use the bucket as soon as they turned out my cell light. Then I heard a voice close to me, from the next cell.

'Be careful of Ikram, and there'll be more like him. They wait for provocation to hurt, so keep your head down. Do not argue or give him a reason to punish you.'

I didn't answer. I wondered why he was in jail.

Ikram arrived with rice and a spoonful of curry on a tin plate. Unfortunately he had to unlock the door to put it inside.

'So you have high and mighty friends. Colonel Rafique.' He sneered as he said the name. 'He thinks he's still in the army, but he's a has-been. He can't touch us.'

He still hadn't locked the door. Strange how I was more concerned that he lock the cell than any thought of escape.

'You'll have to stay here tonight.' He said it conversationally, but I wasn't fooled by his assumed manner. 'Too risky to shift you right now.' He moved closer and his shadow fell on me.

I'd heard of girls being raped in police stations. Could that happen here? I pulled my dupatta closer around me. I wished I had a shawl. For the first time I even wished I wore a burqa.

'How old are you, I wonder? You are not a child – children don't look full and ripe like you do.' He grunted. 'Young, maybe, but you're probably not even pure.'

The thought of defending myself rose up and I opened my mouth but I remembered in time the prisoner's advice. I forced myself not to be goaded. What if it didn't work? If I screamed, would the senior officer come to my aid? Or was I not worth their care? I shut my eyes. Ikram's breathing came closer. He must have been on his haunches, then he stood. 'You'll keep.'

I glanced up as he locked the door, and wished I hadn't. He gave me that evil smirk. It made me want to bathe myself.

The light went out but I waited until I thought the prisoner was asleep; then I washed myself in the bucket of water after I'd drunk my fill. Afterwards, I used the empty bucket. There was a lota, a plastic jug to wash myself. It was so degrading to be kept where there were no other women.

I slept fitfully on the cement floor. They didn't even give me a blanket to lie on. Every door-slam woke me. The mob outside grew quiet.

In the early hours of the next morning after the call of the azan my cell was unlocked.

'Get up!' It was a new officer.

When I stood he handcuffed me and chained me to his belt so that I was forced to walk beside him out of the cell.

'Keep quiet,' he hissed even though I hadn't made a sound.

There were other officers standing to attention near a rear door. A new senior officer frowned at me. 'I'm sending you to a district jail in the Punjab where you will wait for your case to come up in court.'

I stared at him in horror. That was a prison. I thought my innocence would be fixed here.

'It has a women's section. There are not many women's jails and nowhere for a girl your age,' he said, sounding annoyed. 'At any rate it will be much too dangerous to keep you in the district jail here in Khyber Pakhtunkhwa.'

He glanced at my face and his expression softened a little. 'You should be safe.'

His words did nothing to reassure me. He tipped his

head at the officer by my side. 'This is Siddique. He is your bodyguard – he will try to keep you alive on the way.'

If Sammy had spoken in that same tone, he would have been joking, but surely this officer wasn't.

I glanced up at Siddique. He was as young as the officer who had stared at me in distaste the night before, but his face was immobile. Only a muscle in his cheek gave any indication that he sensed my interest. There was no warmth or care in his features. I could have been a buffalo he had to guard, not someone's daughter. Though it could have been worse – he could have been Ikram.

CHAPTER

14

We travelled south. The district jail was only a few hours away. Maybe I would be close to Hadassah. My cotton school uniform wasn't warm enough in the early morning and I couldn't wrap my arms around myself. Without a shawl to cover myself, I felt so exposed sitting next to Siddique, my hands cuffed behind me so I couldn't brace myself from our thighs touching when the police van turned corners. It was like a macabre joining of a man and a girl with no joy on either side. Just like a shy groom, he didn't speak once, and I was relieved – it was better than unwanted attention.

After the traffic became heavier and the van took more turns I could see a huge sand-coloured building with white doors. It looked like a castle. There was a crowd outside, the men shouting and raising fists when they saw the police van. Siddique banged on the partition for the driver to keep going, but there were men gathered around the back too.

'Shit!' He unlocked my handcuffs. 'You'll walk better without these but you must stay close beside me. Do you understand?'

I nodded as he locked my wrist chain loosely to his belt. 'This is for your safety.'

The van stopped close to the building and men jumped out of the way. Siddique opened the back door. It didn't take long for the crowd from the front to materialise before us. The men's shouts of 'Kill her, kill her' rushed around me until I thought I'd faint.

Siddique stood in front of me, scanning the crowd. Then he shouted at them, 'Go home! Go back to work! There is nothing for you here.'

'We want to see her!'

'Ji, we want to see the blasphemer!'

The men behind jostled the ones in front and Saddique pulled out his pistol. He shot it in the air and two things happened. The men fell quiet for a moment and a dozen police in khaki uniforms and assault rifles appeared in a marching run to stand around the van, forming a path into the jail.

Siddique pulled me and we hurried past the riot police, his arm around my back, keeping me on the path.

'You shouldn't protect a blasphemer,' one man shouted as the clamour started up again. The men in fatigues edged closer to the crowd but I didn't see what happened after that, for we were inside the building.

Siddique delivered me to a room bigger than the police station. He reported to the jail superintendant with me still in tow. I was so unnerved by the mob that by then my whole body was shaking. Siddique glanced at me and, for the first time, I saw a flicker of compassion in his eyes.

A large female officer appeared beside us and Siddique unchained me. She dismissed him with a nod and asked me to state my name and my crime to the superintendant sitting behind a desk. I didn't speak; I didn't want to say what I was accused of.

She came closer and the look on her face made me open my mouth. 'My name is Aster Suleiman Masih, I am accused of blasphemy.'

The officer slapped me hard across the face, harder than any Mrs Abdul had given me. I grabbed my glasses as they fell.

'Stupid girl! I don't want to know what you're accused of, just state your name and your crime.'

I glanced behind me, hoping Siddique would step in. Wasn't he supposed to be my bodyguard? But he was gone. I was shocked at how bereft that made me feel. The man behind the desk watched me impassively, as if I was a stray mouse in a cage.

'But I'm not guilty.'

Her next slap made me stagger and I put a foot back to stay on my feet. This time I kept my glasses in my hand. It was strange how I could still think about keeping my glasses safe.

'Say it!' she screamed.

'My name is Aster Suleiman Masih and my crime is blasphemy.' I hesitated over 'my crime' and she made me say it again. The next time I didn't say it loud enough. She shouted at me to say it louder. I said it again and again, and each time the humiliation rose higher, swamping me. If I said it enough times, would I believe it? Is that what this was for?

The superintendant finally waved his hand and the officer stopped badgering me. Would they interrogate me now? Slap me some more? I already had a headache.

She wrote on a slate and smirked as she showed me. 'This states who you are now and your crime. Remember it.'

I put my glasses on, hoping she wouldn't hit me anymore. The chalk gave my number: 753, the date, June 9th, my name in Urdu and the number of my crime: 295C.

'Hold it, 753,' she said. She pinned a piece of cloth with the number 753 on my qameez, then took a photo. I felt like a monkey in a zoo, exhibit A.

After hours of forms and questions and interminable waiting, I was finally told how to conduct myself in the jail. The officer read from a folder: no phones, no computers or devices that connected to the internet, no social media. I could write letters but they would be censored and could be used as evidence. I signed the page where her fat thumb indicated without a murmur. It was hot and I hadn't even been given a drink of water. But I had learned not to ask.

The guard chained me to her belt and marched me out of the room and down a corridor. She moved faster than I thought she would. At my eye level a patch of sweat spread from under her arm. There were men in the cells, putting their hands out; one actually managed to touch me. The officer took up a lot of room in the corridor. I wondered how she grew so big. No one in our village had extra food to put on so much weight. She was like a fat genie I'd seen in a picture book. We finally came to the women's corridor. Some of the women watched me quietly, but one shouted, 'Hey, kid, what are you doing in here?'

'Are you visiting?' another said and the others laughed.

The genie unchained me, then opened the door of a cell packed with women like the ones we'd passed, and pushed me inside.

'Welcome to hell,' one woman hissed at me.

Another jumped in front of me on all fours like a baboon. She giggled, but it was an unnerving sound. One young woman even had a little child with her. The mother didn't look much older than me. There were two bunk beds woven with plastic cord – our charpais at home were woven with hemp rope – and thin cane mats piled up against one wall. One of the bunk beds had three layers.

I was hungry but no one gave me food. It was afternoon by then and I'd missed both breakfast and lunch. A bucket of water and a container to drink with stood in a corner near the door but I didn't want to annoy the women, who were probably all Muslim. I must have been staring at the bucket, for the girl with the child brought me a tin mug of water. I thanked her and she sat cross-legged in front of me with the toddler.

'Isn't that a school uniform?'

The little girl crawled across her mother's legs to sit in my lap. If she had always lived in this cell, she probably thought she had five mothers. What was one more?

I tipped my head at the young mother, aware of the women nearby, listening.

'What's your name? Mine's Kamilah Muhammad.'

'My name is Jani,' the child said. She was very solemn but she dragged my plait to the front of her and inspected the ribbon at the end of it. 'Neela, blue,' she said.

Her mother was staring at me, chewing something in her mouth. It looked like a piece of gum. Where would she get that in here?

I was wary. If I gave my full name, they'd all know my religion. And what if they thought the same as the mob outside the school? Some of the women shuffled closer, sitting in a semicircle behind Kamilah.

'Aster,' I said quickly.

'That's a different name,' Kamilah said. 'What are you doing here if you're a schoolgirl? You must be the youngest prisoner in the prison.'

I shifted under her direct gaze, smarting from the label 'prisoner'. Surely I'd be let out as soon as they discovered this was a mistake?

Jani was undoing the ribbon. In normal circumstances I'd give it to her; I had plenty more at home. But I might need it here. She murmured my name over and over – Aster, Aster, Aster until it became Asti. She smiled at me but I couldn't return it. The nickname made me think of my little cousins.

An older woman with a voice like stones rolling together called out. 'Answer the question! Why are you here? Zina, adultery?'

I shook my head in horror. It must have showed, for Kamilah's face changed; her eyes narrowed. 'It's too easy to get accused of zina.'

A woman with an acid scar on her cheek spoke, 'Kamilah was accused of zina but she was forced, of course. When the baby began to show she was reported to the police.'

'Guess who reported her?' said the woman with the voice of stones.

I shook my head. *How could I know?*

'Her own father.'

I stared at Kamilah in shock and she looked appeased.

'Ji, this is the life we have. Do you think I could find four male witnesses to testify I was forced?'

I could never imagine my father doing that to me.

'The last woman who birthed a baby in here had a boy – the family took him away.' The older woman spat on the floor. 'The honour of the family! But what use is honour when innocent girls go to jail?'

She pointed to the woman who crouched on all fours. 'Narjis was married to a cruel warlord to pay off a debt and she ran away.'

She swept her arm in a circle to encompass the cell. 'All of us here are innocent.'

'Except me, Gazaalah.' The young woman with the scar stared the older woman down.

'Ji, except you, Durrah,' Gazaalah mumbled.

The older woman was nothing like a gazelle, no deer-like qualities in her voice or form at all. People's names could be surprising.

'And I'd do it again.' Durrah's stare was piercing. 'The way he used me, and his mother was no better – they were going to kill me, but no one believed me.' Her voice ended in a shout and I moved further against the wall, my arms around the child, Jani, who wasn't perturbed at all.

'So what do they think you did?' Kamilah persisted with me.

They were all watching me, even Narjis. 'I made a mistake in an exam.' I would not say that word, 'blasphemy'. The woman with the scar would beat me for sure.

Kamilah frowned. 'That's no reason to go to jail.'

'That's what I did.'

Durrah shouted at me. 'What did you do? Tell the truth!'

I stared at her, wondering how to say it. *Truth?* In our country if you tell the truth, you die.

Just then the genie slowed as she passed the cell. She said two words, 'Masihi blasphemer.'

She sounded as smug as if she'd found me out herself. I held my breath. Would the women turn into monsters like the mob of men outside?

Gazaalah shifted closer, frowning at me.

'What subject was it?' She was getting closer to the truth of it. 'Tell us.'

'Islamiyat.'

'Ahh,' she said as if I had explained everything, 'and you insulted the Prophet.'

Instantly all the women stilled, and I felt as if I had to save myself. 'The teacher says I did, but I must have spelt a word wrong.'

The silence continued and a few women glanced at a woman who hung her head in the cell next to ours.

'Too bad. Hafsah there,' Gazaalah pointed to the woman, 'she's in prison for blasphemy too.'

I felt a lurch in my stomach. Maybe I wouldn't be the only Christian. I turned towards Hafsah and said quietly, 'Are you Masihi?'

But all the women heard me.

'Of course she's not!' Gazaalah said. 'Do you think people have to be Hindu, Masihi or Ahmadi to get accused of blasphemy? There are more Muslims accused than anyone else.'

I stared at her, astounded.

'Hafsah is Muslim.' She shouted at the woman called Hafsah. 'Tell her, tell this Masihi Aster how you got accused.'

Hafsah was young, maybe only twenty. But she seemed tired. She spoke, but I imagined it was only the force of Gazaalah's personality that made her open her mouth.

'I was bringing in quilts after airing,' she said, as if she'd related this a hundred times. 'I had to lift them higher to not knock glasses from a table. But the top one caught the Holy Qur'an on its high shelf. It fell and landed so close to the fire that a corner was burned.'

'But that's just an accident! How—'

Hafsah didn't answer. Just then the food came on a tray. The genie shoved it into the cell, and the women quickly crowded around it. There were seven chapattis and a bowl of curry in the middle to share. I was shoved backwards. I wasn't sure if it was on purpose or accidental so I gingerly edged closer. One woman who hadn't spoken yet saw me and threw down her chapatti.

'I'll not eat out of the same dish as a kafir. She'll defile it and how can we wash ourselves properly in here?'

'Chup, Muneerah!' Gazaalah said. 'Keep eating, she can have hers last.'

I sighed. Would they leave me any? I felt my eyes prickling. If only my parents knew, but what could they do?

When Muneerah finished she walked over and slapped me on the side of my face. The force of it threw me backwards and my head hit the bars behind me; my glasses landed on the floor.

'I don't care what the others say about sisterhood and innocence, I don't want a blasphemer here.'

Surprisingly I found the courage to answer, 'I'm not one.'

'Tell me you believe Muhammad, Peace be Upon Him, is the last Prophet.'

I kept my mouth shut. Whatever I said, she would take it the wrong way. How could a non-Muslim answer that question without offense?

'See?' She turned to the others. 'They all say they're innocent but where there's mud there's been rain.'

She turned back to me. 'A teacher wouldn't accuse you unless you were guilty.'

She gave me another slap, as hard as the genie's. The pain seared through my head and I cowered, tensed for the next one.

'Muneerah, leave her alone!'

Muneerah faced Gazaalah. 'Who's going to tell?' She looked around the cell. 'She deserves to die. That's the law. I'd be rewarded, maybe I'll be freed. I could even earn a place in heaven. There'll be a price on her head soon by some mullah, if there isn't already. Imagine what the Taliban would do to her – stone her, probably.'

At that Gazaalah reached up and pulled me away from Muneerah. She lifted her chin at the tray. 'Eat what's left.'

The other women watched me. There was one chapatti and about two mouthfuls of vegetable curry. Did they forget to leave me enough or, like Muneerah, did they think I didn't deserve it?

It was difficult eating under their watchful gaze, wondering if someone else would hit me. I scooped up the curry in pieces of chapatti but it stuck in my throat. I felt it would surge up and I'd vomit. I tried calming myself, thinking of the village, the platefuls of sweet rice we had at Hadassah's wedding, and crawled to find a space as far away from Muneerah as I could to finish the rest of the chapatti in peace.

I found myself close to Kamilah, who handed me my glasses but didn't speak to me. Maybe if Muneerah heard her, she'd beat her too. She sang in a low voice to Jani and cuddled her. It suddenly struck me: she could have been Hadassah. If anyone in town had known Hadassah's secret and told the police, she would have been arrested and sent to jail too. We had no male witness, let alone four. Only I saw what happened and considering I was a girl and too naïve at the time to understand, my testimony was worth nothing.

It was hot in the cell with no fan. There was also no toilet, just a hole in the cement floor. Our village courtyard was like this but I expected more from an institution like a jail. Again I wished I had a shawl, not only to keep myself warm when the nights would get cooler but to shield myself when using the hole, but it had to be done.

No one remarked, though I caught Durrah and Muneerah watching me. Were they checking I cleaned myself properly?

At least there was a cane mat for me, but hardly any floor space to put it, and no spare blanket.

The corridor fell quiet as the evening wore on, and I lay on the mat, as close as possible to Kamilah's bunk bed, my glasses by me on the floor. What if it got cooler in the early morning? I could imagine the slap the genie would give me if I asked for a blanket. I tried to keep my weeping quiet.

This was a nightmare. The mobs of men, the riot police. Would it have been on the news? *What must Ammi and Abba be thinking?* Were they safe? The whole village would weep and pray, but were my parents still in the village or had they fled? I tried to pray, but my mind kept jumping like young goats. How annoying I had thought them when I had to round them up for the night. My heart beat too loudly when I lay on my left side so I rolled to the other.

Then I remembered the story of Yusef and his multi-coloured coat. He was betrayed by his brothers, just as Kamilah was by her family. And me: it was Mrs Abdul who put me here. I didn't want to think about her – those thoughts would turn into demons and gnaw at me from the inside.

Yusef, think about Yusef instead – he ended up in jail. He did his best to honour Khuda even under the threat of death and became respected by the prison guards. For years he waited for someone to remember he was imprisoned.

How long will I be here? Yusef had a special talent for interpreting dreams. That was how he was released and became Governor of Egypt, second only to Pharaoh. But I had no special talent, nothing with which to save myself.

MESSAGES

Sammy Ibrahim, + 3 Salaam, cousins. Perhaps you know already our tragic news. Aster has been accused of blasphemy. Something to do with her exams. There was a riot outside the Government Girls High School yesterday. The army had to disperse the crowd. Her parents, Uncle Suleiman and Aunty Marya, are so shocked but they can't do anything to help. Even Colonel Rafique couldn't get bail for her. Please pray for us.

Hadassah Bashir I am so sorry for this. Please tell Aunty and Uncle we are thinking of them.

Sammy Ibrahim It gets worse. There have been death threats, not only against Aster but also her family, which is actually the whole village. We are packing in case the village is torched. Aster has been moved to a district jail for her own safety. So far we don't know where she is.

Hadassah Bashir Tell Aunty and Uncle they can stay with my new family.

Afia Yunis Hie, this is awful news. People can stay in our village too.

Maryam Yusef I wish I could say you could come to Australia and stay with us but no such luck with our strict refugee policy, I'm afraid. I will write on my blog. Will you all visit and sign a petition to free Aster?

Afia Yunis Will that work, Maryam?

Maryam Yusef We have to do something to let the government there understand that people around the world know about it. We all love Pakistan, but do we want injustice like this happening? Where is the freedom for minorities that's promised in the constitution?

Sammy Ibrahim This doesn't just happen to minorities either.

Maryam Yusef Something needs to be changed. How can I contact Aster? Do they have internet in Pakistani prisons?

Hadassah Bashir My husband Danyal says no internet is allowed. No phones either. You could write a letter, but be careful. It will be censored.

Sammy Ibrahim I'll let you know when we know which jail. It's probably in the Punjab.

Maryam Yusef I'll write on Aster's wall so her friends know.

Peacock Blue I've heard Peacock Blue has been arrested for blasphemy. I am her cousin, Maryam from Australia, and I think it's unbelievable that this can be true – that an innocent minor can be accused of such a thing. If you would like to help her please click on the link to see my blog and to sign a petition.

Like · Comment · Share

Step by Step
To see a world where freedom, peace and justice reign

Free Peacock Blue

A fourteen-year-old village schoolgirl does an Islamic exam and her teacher accuses her of blasphemy. A riot ensues and she is jailed. Is this the land of the pure we love and honour? How threatened the minority communities must feel? How much pressure laid on the police and legal system by religious extremists? How is the girl treated? Think of the terror she must feel, an innocent victim. We'll call her Peacock Blue for her safety.

Last year another girl was accused of blasphemy for burning pages of the Qur'an while she collected rubbish. She was given bail when it was discovered that a mullah had planted the pages in her path. The girl couldn't read and would not have distinguished a Qur'anic page from any other. The bail was excessive, yet the money came from overseas organisations horrified by the girl's plight. It was the first time bail was given for blasphemy in Pakistan. I have read that bail will not be given in Peacock Blue's case as the evidence against her is apparently 'strong'. I hope this petition will help her. Join with me in signing this petition to the governor of Punjab to please free my cousin, Peacock Blue. Sign <u>here</u>

COMMENTS

Ahmed Assalamu Alaikum, sister ji. This never used to happen before ex-President Zia changed the law to include the death sentence. This law needs to be reformed to exclude the death sentence.

Fatima Anyone who has tried to reform that law has been killed by extremists. No one wants to touch it.

Shafique This is sad news, but it is happening more and more. It won't stop until they start prosecuting the people who wrongfully accuse others. God bless you, sister, for doing this for your cousin.

Abdulla This girl deserves the punishment she will surely receive. Islam must be respected and Sharia law upheld. I hope she gets the death penalty.

Affat Shame on you, Abdulla. Where is your love? And is our God so small we have to protect him from a child? I am Muslim too but comments like yours do damage to Islam and give our faith a bad name. All thoughtful Muslims will abhor this treatment of a fourteen-year-old schoolgirl.

Abdulla There are already demonstrations calling for this evil girl's death.

Fozia Religion always causes problems. I'm an atheist and I live in a progressive country where no one cares about religion. Nothing like this can happen.

Tamsin I agree religions cause trouble, especially ones built on inflexible rituals and rules which open the way to prejudice. I believe God prefers a relationship with us; he's about mercy not religion, grace not rules.

Habib That's crap – the priests wouldn't be able to control what everyone thought if you had a religion like that. People might get it wrong.

Tamsin I rest my case.

Affat Fozia, if you lived in a country like mine that has a state religion, you'd be put in jail for not believing. That also can be called blasphemy. We need to stand together for freedom to believe what we want, or not to believe, without threat of violence.

CHAPTER

15

I'm in prison in a solitary cell. No toilet, no water, the floor stinks of goat manure and the food smells like fish that's been on the Karachi train in summer. I can see through the bars and I see Yusef riding past in his chariot – he does this every day, watching the wheat crops, giving orders for harvesting and where to keep the grain to feed Egypt through the seven-year drought. I bang on the bars. 'Lord Yusef, save me. You were innocent like I am. Tell the king to free me.' But he never hears me. Now when I call, the bars move closer together. When I lie on my mat the ceiling descends a few inches. Then a few more. I will be squashed.

I sprang awake but it was too early. The cell was dark and I could hear one of the women snoring; I imagined it was Gazaalah. The aftermath of the dream brought shadows that flickered at the edges of my mind and I wondered how my parents were. How shocked they must be. How wonderful it would be to see them, to know they were safe.

As I lay there thinking, I realised something horrifying: I couldn't feel God. Was my faith only something I believed in my happy life in the village? Then I heard Abba in my head: *Khuda is always with us whether we feel He is or not, just believe.*

I sighed and thought about the village – Gudiya and her soft brown eyes, the goats, the land and wheatfields, sunrise, sunset, singing in church, the laughing of children – there was so much colour, brightness and light. Except for the chipped green bars, there were no colours here; it was like looking out a window and seeing nothing, just blankness. This prison was every shade of grey.

How did it come to this? Had the Colonel reported Mrs Abdul after all? Was that why she never let up on me?

I told myself that regardless of squashed dreams I had to think beyond these barred walls. Yet still I wept until little Jani woke and used the hole. Then she curled up beside me.

'We must sit on the mats soon for breakfast,' she whispered.

'Teik hai.' I wiped my face with my dupatta, I had nothing else.

The women woke. Narjis, the one who had jumped like a monkey when I was pushed into the cell the day before, crawled over to us. She sat on her haunches watching me, her head on the side. Then she called me 'daughter'.

'Beti, can you see the forest, the trees?' She indicated the cell. 'We are in a forest – see the monkey up there on the branch?'

I looked up at a qameez hanging on the rope to dry. So did Jani.

'See it?'

I nodded to humour her. 'Ji.'

'Ji,' Jani said as if she really could see it.

'It's laughing at you.'

I glanced at her quickly. 'Why?'

'Because you know how to laugh and sing and you don't do it now. It doesn't matter if we are in the forest or on a dangerous mountain path, we can laugh.'

Narjis took my hands and clapped them as I'd done to babies many times. She sang a funny song about a monkey and a jackal fighting over a bone. Jani quickly joined in, Kamilah too. Jani even smiled as she clapped.

I thought Muneerah would jump down and slap us but she watched from her bed as if she were bemused. That was when I realised the other women tolerated Narjis as people tolerate mad holy people, as if God's favour is on them.

When the song was finished, Narjis leaned in closer and pinched my cheek. 'You mustn't forget the good things.'

She moved away and I squeezed my eyes shut, trying to imagine the cell as my home. My charpai was over there, where I slept and did my homework, the computer on the low table, the rug Dadi-ji wove from rags on the floor in the middle. The trunk with my folded clothes. I imagined taking out the shalwar qameez Juli Rafique gave me, laying it on a sheet on the rug and ironing out the creases. Was Narjis only imagining like this, or did she really believe she was in a happier place, the jungle of her childhood? I looked up to find her watching me. Her smile was too wild but she nodded at me as if I'd been a good girl.

After the food came and we'd eaten – me last again – Jani asked for a story. My dream was still playing in my head so I began telling her about Yusef and his dreams. I'd told it to Sammy's siblings many times. I swallowed down the memories and began, 'Yusef had a gift from Khuda, he could interpret dreams. One day the king had a dream about seven skinny cows and seven fat ones, and he wanted to know what it meant.

'The cup-bearer finally remembered Yusef, who was in prison, and brought him before the king.

'"I hear you can interpret dreams," the king asked, but Yusef said, "Only Khuda can do this but if you tell me the dream, I will ask Him what it means."'

Suddenly my head was jerked backwards – Muneerah had me by the hair.

'Tell a different story,' she hissed. 'I know what you're doing, you're telling about your religion, little blasphemer.'

'Many Bible stories are also in the Qur'an.'

But I got a slap for answering back. Muneerah probably didn't even know what was in the Qur'an. I ducked my head to shield my glasses.

'Tell a different one, a story about jinns and animals.'

I fell quiet and Muneerah left me alone. Mrs Rafique had given Ijaz and me a storybook of folktales and finally

I remembered one to tell Jani. Sammy had thought it so funny. 'This is about a jackal who outwitted a hungry tiger by luring him to walk into a cage.'

I'd barely started when a guard I hadn't seen before appeared outside the cell. He swaggered as though he was the most important guard in the prison. He scrutinised us in the cell until his gaze fell on me.

'You, 753!' He lifted his chin at me. 'Out!'

'Oooh, you have Green Eyes to escort you, lucky girl.' Gazaalah's voice dripped with sarcasm as some of the women laughed, not very kindly.

The man was middle-aged and his stomach hung over his belt like a sack of flour. His only redeeming feature was his eyes – when he chose to open them wide enough – for they were indeed green. He unlocked the cell but I didn't move fast enough for him. He reached in and yanked me out. Kamilah held Jani close to her as she watched him drag me out the door and slam it shut. She didn't smirk like Muneerah.

'Karam will pull you in line, blasphemer,' Muneerah called after me.

Karam was another person ill-named, for Karam means kindness. His whole body stank, his breath too. He shackled me to his belt but he took too long over it and his hand caressed the side of my waist. There was nothing I could say or do. I was at his mercy while I was chained to him. He marched down the corridor while I tried to keep up, worried sick that I was to be interrogated. Would they interrogate a schoolgirl? And my biggest fear: would I become Muslim because I couldn't stand the pain?

All the way Karam leered at me, past the cells of women, through a double door, then another corridor of men prisoners who called out, 'Hey gudyia, doll,' or 'Hoori, angel,' as if I were a Bollywood actress. Karam's swagger grew and his leg kept brushing my thigh. I was sure it was on purpose. The prisoner in the police station was right: there would be someone else like Ikram.

We finally reached a room. Karam opened the door and pushed me in with his hand on my backside. I wished I could have said, 'Sharam, shame on you.' If I had been in a street in town I would have taken off my shoe and hit him with it. He'd be so ashamed, he'd never touch me again. But I couldn't do that here. He'd retaliate for sure and I had no recourse. Besides, who would believe me or care? Even the women in the cell had watched with glee when he took me away, happy it wasn't them. Except Kamilah – she'd looked worried.

Karam unlocked the chain, without touching me this time, and stood against the wall.

I looked up to see who my visitor was and felt glad he hadn't seen my shame as Karam pushed me in. It was Dr Amal. The relief almost made me fall. He had his back to me, looking through his bag.

Karam cleared his throat. 'The prisoner 753 is delivered.'

Dr Amal swung around, pulling an ear bud from his ear. 'Aster, are you okay?'

I nodded, flabbergasted in his presence as I always was when he visited the village.

'I came to see how you are. Please, sit.' He indicated a chair on the other side of a table. I glanced at Karam but he didn't shake his head. I saw a stamp like a tattoo that said 'Visitor' on Dr Amal's forearm.

'They don't seem to want you to have visitors,' he said at first.

'How did you get in?'

'I said I was your family doctor.'

I dropped my gaze under his and wondered if they believed him – girls my age didn't go to male doctors.

'So, how are you?'

He didn't mean if I was sick; I knew he wanted to know how I was coping.

My eyes stung. 'I wish I was home.'

Dr Amal glanced at Karam and lowered his voice. 'I know where your parents are. I've seen them—'

I cut in, 'How are they? They haven't been hurt?' The noise of the mob at the police station replayed often in my mind.

'They are well and send their love and blessings. They are on their way to your cousin Hadassah.' He paused, then added, 'They are distressed of course, we all are, but it is too dangerous for them to come.'

His eyes watered but he controlled himself and handed me a parcel. 'This is from your parents.'

It had been opened, probably by the guards, and I could see a shalwar qameez and my mother's warm shawl. I forced myself to be polite and not to touch it yet but it took my breath away to have something of hers so close.

'And this is from my family.' It wasn't wrapped and I gasped in relief. It was a lightweight cotton shawl for summer and although it was a gift I couldn't help myself; I put it on immediately, over my head and tucked under my chin. It was a large one used for purdah and when I stood I knew it would be as long as my qameez. 'How did they know I'd need this?'

'My mother visits our local jail. You can use the warmer one in your parents' parcel as a blanket.'

My eyes filled from the kindness and perception of both family and strangers. 'A shawl is what I need the most. There was no time—' I stopped as his hand hovered over mine but he shifted it to take something from his pocket.

He took out a scarf. 'I also have brought a gift. I remember how you like to sing. It's in here.' He indicated the scarf in his hand. 'It's the old CD Walkman I had before my iPod. Sorry, there's only one CD. I didn't want to push it. Keep it hidden from your cellmates.' His voice was low as he slipped it into the parcel of clothes with some spare batteries. I hoped Karam didn't notice.

I managed to get the Walkman safely to the cell and didn't take it out until the light went off that night. Having the Walkman was the first bit of excitement other than seeing Dr Amal since my arrest. My fingers were shaking as I put the ear buds in and pressed a button.

Suddenly my head was flooded with sound. Dr Amal's songs. 'Umeed' was the first one. 'You are my hope,' he sang. I lay on my mat, imagining I was back in the village, in my room after the talks Dr Amal had given, after Sammy and I had led the singing.

When I felt sleepy I turned it off. I'd have to listen sparingly, for the batteries wouldn't last forever. What would I do then? I squeezed it halfway into my qameez pocket, wrapped the cotton shawl around me and fell asleep on my mother's shawl. It smelt of her jasmine oil.

CHAPTER

16

Ijaz is outside in the field. He's laughing, and not using the scythe correctly. Sammy shows him how. A jeep burns up the lane and men in black shirts and khaki trousers with AK47 Kalashnikovs jump out. They take Ijaz; the scythe falls and cuts his leg. He is bleeding yet still they drag him away.

'We'll be back for you,' one says to me.

I run after them, screaming for them to bring him back, 'He's innocent!'

I woke to Kamilah patting my face. 'Shhh,' she said. 'You'll wake the others, and they'll beat you.'

It was almost light in the cell. I sat up and tried to slow my breathing.

'You were dreaming,' she whispered. 'Jani does that too. Muneerah slapped both of us last time. No one likes being woken.'

When she felt satisfied I wouldn't make another noise

she said, 'Come up to our bed, but be careful, don't wake Gazaalah.'

I followed her up to the top bunk, missing Gazaalah's hands on the way. Kamilah lay down, her arm around Jani, and whispered for me to lie down beside them.

Her eyes were open, watching me. 'It takes a long time to settle. I still miss my home, my family, my animals. I was going to be married, but he will have married someone else now. I carried his photo from when I was thirteen.'

She smiled but it was a sad one. 'When I get out of here I will be old.'

'When will you be released?'

She made a face. 'I don't know. There has been no hearing of my case. No one would pay bail either. What will be the point of getting out anyway? My family won't want me. At least Jani is fed in here.'

'But you can't give up.'

Kamilah raised her head. 'See if you can say that to me when you've been in here five years.'

I took her meaning and shut my mouth. I needed prison guidelines. Knowing what to say to cellmates is not something you learn at school or home. I closed my eyes, praying I wouldn't have another nightmare. When I opened them again, an hour must have passed. It was light.

Jani was pulling my plait. 'Asti, wake up.'

The nickname still hurt – when would I see Sammy's little sisters and brother again?

'Asti? We eat now.' Her speech was harder to understand than my young cousins'. She probably didn't get much practice. I could imagine the other women telling her to shut up if she spoke too much.

I rolled over and stared at her. She pulled on my hands. 'Up, up.'

Kamilah whispered, 'Get up now. The guard will come.' She sounded worried.

All the women were sitting on their mats on the floor, waiting. Then I heard the sound of a trolley. Doors were opened and shut until it was our turn. The genie unlocked the door. She dropped a tray on the floor with cups and an aluminium pot of chai. Then she threw in a cane tray with chapattis and a pot of what looked like leftover curry from the night before. I thought of the food we had at home, of vegetable curries that were rich in flavour and hot with chilli.

The genie unlocked Hafsah's door and there was an exclamation, 'You lazy slut, get up!'

She walked in with a tin plate of food and yanked Hafsah out of the bed, then slapped her across the face. Hafsah's head hit the bars of our cell and everyone watched, our food untouched. Kamilah tried to hide Jani's face against her chest.

'You think you're a queen to be waited on in your special bedroom?' She slapped Hafsah again.

Finally Hafsah said, 'Sorry, so tired.'

'You wouldn't be tired if you ate food. Now eat!' The genie waited until Hafsah had taken a mouthful. She choked but the genie seemed satisfied and locked the cell. Now I understood Jani's worry that I wasn't sitting on my mat for breakfast.

'She gets what she deserves,' Mumeerah muttered and the women began eating. I still had to wait until last.

Kamilah whispered to me, 'When I was new, they used to make me eat after everyone else too.'

'But you're Muslim.'

'It has nothing to do with religion, but who is the boss. This cell is a farmyard.'

When it was my turn to eat there was more left this time. Did it help not to retaliate? It was difficult to know how to behave.

Kamilah put the trays in the corner by the door. I was dying to go to the toilet by now, but still embarrassed about doing it in full view of the women in the cell. What did they do? I hadn't seen anyone except Jani use that hole in the daytime.

The trolley edged its way up the corridor, picking up the trays. I was just building up the nerve to use the hole when the genie unlocked our door again. The women all stood. She chained us all together by threading a chain through the ones on our wrists. Kamilah held Jani. First was Gazaalah, who was chained to the genie and we all followed.

No one seemed worried, so our destination couldn't be a torture room.

We reached a washroom at the end of the corridor. The chain was yanked from our arms. Someone called and the genie stepped outside, leaving the door ajar. The room stank but we could go to the squat toilet, have a shower and wash our clothes in troughs. If I'd known, I could have brought the shalwar qameez my parents sent to me and changed out of my school clothes, but I soon got over the disappointment of no fresh clothes, for squatting over a proper toilet in the floor with a cubicle around felt good even with the toilet overflowing with excrement. It looked as if the cleaner hadn't been in yet.

The shower was cold – which didn't matter in summer – but there were no spare towels. The one on a hook stank of mildew and unimaginable filth. After removing my under-wear I showered in my shalwar qameez and let myself dry. I couldn't bring myself to use that vile towel.

At the troughs Kamilah had some of Jani's clothes and a shalwar qameez of her own to wash. She showed me what to do. 'This is the detergent that we wash clothes in. Here's the soap.'

She lifted Jani into a trough and washed her and the clothes at the same time.

'We may be in prison,' she said, 'but my child will be clean.' She rubbed soap into Jani's hair while she protested.

Durrah pushed me away from Kamilah just as I was about to turn the water on in the next trough. 'I always use this one.'

I wondered if she did, but how could I know what to do? Sammy was in my head suddenly and said, *Challenge her back. It's just a test.*

Gazaalah was observing me. I walked to the trough on the other side of Kamilah. Muneerah was suddenly there as if she had been waiting for my next move. Like a cobra strike, she belted me across the head. The force of it put me flat on my back on the cement and I heard the shattering of glass. For a moment I couldn't move.

Winded, Sammy said.

I'd never been beaten like this. I managed to sit up to check my head. Had it hit the floor? I couldn't remember. I found my glasses but one lens was broken. At least I could still see with my left eye. There wasn't any blood on the floor, but I could taste it in my mouth.

I wanted to shout, *Why did you do this?* Then I remembered: I was just a blasphemer to them.

I had to be careful. We were in a room without a guard, even though I could hear voices outside the door. Whatever happened wouldn't be seen.

The man in the police station had said to keep my head down. I thought he was only talking about men but maybe it would work on Muneerah too. This was the kind of bullying Sammy must have endured at high school. Until he showed them how he could play soccer.

No soccer here.

How could I wash my clothes if the women wouldn't let me? Kamilah, Gazaalah and Narjis had kept out of it and all the other troughs were being used now.

The genie put her head around the door. 'Five minutes.'

I went to Kamilah and she moved to one side so I could put my underwear in the trough to wash with hers. She glanced at me. Her eyes seemed to ask how I was and I tilted my head slightly. I hung onto the edge of the trough with the chain clanging against the side. I wrung out my undies with Durrah's elbow in my ribs.

How would I survive this? How should I react? All the women were bigger than me. I would never win in a fight; I wouldn't even know the first thing to do.

Kamilah smiled at me. 'There's a cupboard under here,' she pointed under the sink, 'where you get pads for your menses.'

Muneerah made a rude noise. 'You won't have to worry about that for long. Prison life will scare your menses away.'

By then my head was hurting so much I could hardly see. The door opened and the genie walked in with the chain. We lined up so she could thread it through our wrist chains again.

That night after I'd changed my clothes on the bunk I lay awake watching the dripping clothes hanging on the rope along the bars of the cell and listening to the Walkman. I dreamed of cages and peacocks. Neelum had been captured by hunters and forced into a cage, but the cage was too small for him to raise his tail. His beautiful fan feathers fell to the floor, then his brown and white underfeathers. Even his crown dropped off. He looked like a plucked bird ready for the pot.

Free Peacock Blue

To see a world where freedom,
peace and justice reign

Sign petition <u>here</u>
Target: 25,000

Children in Jails

Did you know that the age of criminal responsibility in Pakistan was seven years of age until last year? Now it's twelve, except for terrorism cases. However, the penal code does say that nothing done by a child between 7 and 12 years is an offence if they have not attained sufficient maturity of understanding to judge the nature and consequence of their conduct. But who is the judge of whether a child is culpable or not?

In our newspaper this week I read of a nine-month-old baby being arrested along with his grandfather and other family members for attempted murder in Pakistan, throwing rocks at gas company officials. Yes, I can hear your exclamations of disbelief. Maybe the age of the baby is why the story actually made it into our Australian news. His grandfather bottle-fed the baby while answering questions from reporters. He said the charges were fabricated because a rival party wanted the accused evicted from their land. Does this sound familiar?

Last year there were over 1400 children in Pakistani jails. Only 165 were convicted, the rest were under trial, their families being too poor to pay the bail price.

Pakistani prison rules state children should be accommodated separately from adults in different jails; they should play sports, and be rehabilitated. However, there is one juvenile jail in the whole nation, and both Karachi and Hyderabad have a Youthful Offenders Industrial School but the rest of the children are kept in adult district and central jails.

Very few girls are arrested, so can you imagine where Peacock Blue is being kept? The juvenile jail will be for boys. She's probably in an adult jail, maybe in a cell with women. Only one prison has a separate dormitory for Christians, so that they won't be persecuted by other prisoners. So what could be happening to Peacock Blue? Her arrest and imprisonment is a disgrace. Help free Peacock Blue now. Sign the petition <u>here</u> or write a letter to the Pakistani High Commissioner or the Governor of the Punjab.

COMMENTS

Abdulla You are just a stupid kafir girl who knows nothing. Blasphemy must be punished. This blog is rubbish and only western fools will believe your shit. If you do not stop this irreligious blog you will get killed.

Maryam People like you give major faiths a bad name, Abdulla. Injustice must be fought wherever it is found.

Ahmed Don't answer fanatical or extremist views. Let's keep this forum for respectful and open-minded discourse.

Tamsin So sorry to hear about this poor girl. I hope she is not suffering too much in prison.

Dana See how they treat their own? If we let these people into Australia, that's how we'll be treated.

Affat Maryam, there are demonstrations by Muslim groups as well as Christian ones here in Karachi and Lahore asking the government to free your cousin. They march against fear, and false accusations of innocent victims. Imams are joining the protests too. We do not want a law that doesn't protect minorities in Pakistan.

Rashid What about the children Australia has in detention centres? Those people have endured prison, war and torture and now end up in a prison. Australia is a wealthy global nation. You of all countries should uphold the rights of the children and safety of all people.

Dana There are nearly 1000 children in detention centres in Australia and you know what? It serves them right for coming illegally.

Tamsin Australia is better than this, or it used to be. When I hear about how asylum seeker children are treated I'm ashamed to say I'm Australian. The fear of others is corrupting our soul.

Maryam I know. Many Australians are upset about these laws. It's a Christian value to liberate people from oppression and injustice, and to provide hospitality to strangers, but Australia no longer upholds these basic human sentiments at government level.

Khalid These are sentiments in Islam also but my family did not receive them, only imprisonment, because we disagreed with the government. At least you can disagree and work for change.

Abdulla Western governments are weak. I live in a western country too. It was my parents' choice to come here, not mine. I would have made a good jihadi but my father was weak and didn't want to be one. He says he saved me from a bad life but jihad is a sure way into heaven if you die while fighting for Islam. Who wouldn't fight knowing that?

Fozia You've been brainwashed, Abdulla. I don't believe in religion but if I did I'd know God wouldn't want people killing each other.

Tamsin Last week some church leaders in our city were arrested for praying quietly in an electorate office to seek the release of these children in detention and to put an end to our treatment of asylum seekers. The magistrate dismissed the charges and said these leaders are an inspiration and a credit to their faith.

MESSAGES
Sammy Ibrahim Be careful, cousin, you may be in free Australia and you feel no one can touch you but some people have long arms. They can force people online to feel fear, to think like them and become violent.

CHAPTER

17

When I woke in the morning the Walkman was gone. I scrabbled on the floor, searching under the bed. Did it drop down? But it would have woken us up, surely. Was it tangled in my shawl? Nothing.

Jani woke. 'What are you doing?'

'I've lost something.'

'What is it?'

'It's a little CD player – with ear buds.' I despaired – she wouldn't know what I meant – but she surprised me.

'Like that?' She pointed at Durrah on the top bunk closest to the wall. Durrah was bobbing her head, the buds in her ears. They had to be mine. Then she stared straight at me as if she had known all along I would see her. Her smile was smug.

I wanted to shout at her to give the Walkman back. It was mine. Never before had I wanted anything so badly. It was the only link to my real life. I didn't want to do nothing, like the other women. Would I have to fight her? Durrah looked very strong – she'd managed to kill her husband. What would she do to me?

I remembered the story I'd finally told Jani about the jackal trying to appear as if he didn't care if the tiger walked into the cage. I forced myself not to confront Durrah. I climbed up and lay beside Jani.

'Don't you want this?' Durrah finally said.

I sat up. Durrah had taken out the ear buds. I wondered if she really wanted the Walkman, or just a reaction from me.

'It's only got Masihi songs on it – you won't like them. I can tell you stories if you give it back.'

'Nay, you sing a song and I'll think about it.'

I licked my lips and glanced around. All the women were watching. I hadn't had breakfast yet – would my voice be scratchy? Durrah was expecting me to not be able to sing at all, to humiliate me. I faced her and sang 'Any dream will do' from the Yusef movie, *Joseph and the Amazing Technicolour Dreamcoat*. I sang it, staring into her eyes as if we were in close combat. There mightn't have been blows but I knew this was as real as David facing Goliath.

When I'd finished, Jani said in childish awe, 'You sound like a Bollywood actress.'

'Her skin's too dark for an actress,' Muneerah said nastily.

Durrah had lost the attention of the others. She unplugged the ear buds and threw the Walkman at me. I caught it in one hand. Playing cricket with Sammy finally had a use. But she didn't return the ear buds. I looked up and her stare was triumphant, even her scar flared. How was I supposed to get them back?

Later that day Gazaalah told me a woman was asking to see me. She seemed to know everything that went on in the women's corridor.

'Green Eyes will collect you.'

She grinned at my horror. Sure enough, he did come to fetch me from the cell. I endured the usual touches and caresses as he fumbled around chaining me to his belt. He'd progressed to saying lewd things.

'Maybe we can be private one day. I know you are wanting to spend some time with me.'

The words were simple but his meaning wasn't innocent at all.

We neared the interview room and I could hear a woman's voice. She sounded bossier than any of our teachers, even Mrs Abdul.

'You can't keep her in here,' she was saying to the genie as we entered. 'She's only fourteen. I want to see the exam she wrote.'

'It's not in her file.' The genie's tone was sullen.

'Then get it, if the teacher still has it. It's stupid to compel Christian kids to take Islamiyat. Of course they'll get it wrong.'

Karam pushed me into the room. The action twisted my arm and I winced.

'Unchain her,' the woman told him. 'What do you think she is – a serial killer? Bring a chair.'

She sat at the table. Karam brought over a chair and his scowl, as he dropped it near the table for me, made him even uglier. He stood to attention by the door as the genie left the room.

The woman was young, wore a dupatta on her head and sat very straight. She gestured to me to sit.

'Assalamu Alaikum,' she said. 'My name is Mrs Jamal Khan, but please call me Mrs Jamal.'

'Wa Alaikum Assalam.' I returned the greeting.

Mrs Jamal saw my bruises and broken glasses immediately. 'Who did this?'

Her question was like a gunshot and I jumped. I wasn't sure what would happen if I told her, so I said nothing. There was also Karam to consider, since he would have heard her question. She didn't speak softly like Dr Amal.

She glanced at him and lowered her voice. 'Did an officer do it?'

'Nahin,' I whispered.

'Another prisoner?'

I stayed silent and she made her own conclusions. 'So you are in a cell with other women?'

This I could answer. 'Ji. Most are nice enough,' I added, thinking of Kamilah.

'Most isn't good enough.' She lifted her chin at Karam. 'See to it she is put in a single cell. She's only a schoolgirl.'

I wondered who she could be. By what authority could she give orders to officers?

'We have none spare. The cells are already overcrowded.' Karam sounded petulant.

'I don't want to hear excuses. Arrange it somehow.'

She turned back to me. 'So you have yourself in a pit of tigers, I see.'

I wanted her to understand. 'I didn't blaspheme.' I brushed at my eyes. I suspected Mrs Jamal would be impatient with tears.

'Listen,' she said. 'A Christian blasphemes just by refusing to say the Kalimah. It's the blasphemy law we need to reform.'

She sounded like my father when he was with my uncles.

'Are you Muslim?' I ventured, even though I knew she must be.

'Certainly. Not all Muslims believe kids like you should be locked up because they can't spell.'

She leaned down to her handbag and took out a notebook and an iPhone. 'Now, I need details. I am your lawyer.'

It took a moment for her statement to sink into my head. *A lawyer?*

'But how can we pay?'

Mrs Jamal gave me her first smile. 'Let's just say the firm I work for has an interest in cases like yours. You are a minor and you will not need to pay.'

It looked like a dangerous occupation to me. 'Thank you, but how can you do this?'

What power could she have? Even a governor and a cabinet minister were assassinated for trying to support people accused of blasphemy. Our whole village went into mourning for them.

'First we must ascertain your innocence.'

She pressed 'record' on her phone. 'Your full name?'

'Aster Suleiman Masih.'

I watched her write 'Aster Suleiman Masih, Student' at the top of her pad with a fountain pen.

'And you did a first-term Year 8 Islamiyat Studies exam?'

'Ji,' I said miserably.

'And your teacher said you blasphemed. Do you know what you wrote?'

'Nahin. She wouldn't tell me. She said it was too disgusting to repeat.'

'You were arrested on the day of the exam?'

'Ji, after the exam – I didn't even eat my lunch.'

Mrs Jamal frowned. 'So soon? She wouldn't have read all the papers, only yours.'

She tapped her notebook. 'You don't know Arabic, do you?'

'Nahin, miss. I didn't learn it in the village school, but I was studying the Bible in Urdu. I've never heard the Qur'an recited in Arabic other than on TV.'

'And your father switches the channel?'

I hung my head, for it was true.

Mrs Jamal sighed. 'It is your right to follow your own faith. It is in our constitution. However, since the blasphemy law was changed in the nineteen-eighties to include the death sentence, we've had thousands of arrests.'

She considered me. 'They need to prosecute the people who wrongly accuse.'

This was an encouraging thought and I said, 'I must have spelt a word wrong but I didn't mean it to be offensive.'

'Of course not. Any educated and sensible person will understand that.'

Her words silenced me. Crowds of men at gates were not made up of sensible, educated people. Would it come to a court case? Those people were supposed to be educated. I had a sinking feeling that education wasn't always what mattered, but conviction. Mrs Abdul was educated but she was convinced I was evil.

'Now, you keep a strong heart, Aster. I'll make sure your parents know how you are, and they can send items you need. There are many people, some leading imams also, who do not agree with this.'

She put the lid on the pen.

'Can my parents visit?'

She regarded me a moment before answering. 'Do not expect your parents to be able to come straightaway.'

There was a dull feeling in the pit of my belly but I had to ask the question. 'How long do you think I will be here?'

Over the years, I had heard of many Christians jailed for blasphemy; my father prayed constantly for their release. A mother, Asia Bibi, was still on death row after five years.

That was the first time Mrs Jamal hesitated, and the first indication of how difficult my situation was.

'Aster, this must be terrifying for you, but I will not lie to save your feelings.'

She watched me, as if gauging how I would react. 'It may be a long time. I have not been able to secure your bail.'

She paused, tapping her notebook. 'I was hoping that since you are a minor, they'd loosen up on the no-bail rule for blasphemy.'

I opened my mouth to protest my innocence again but she cut me off. 'If you are released now, some people may take it upon themselves to exercise justice. You are safer in here. Also,' she paused, 'your village has been threatened.'

Coils of fear tightened around my chest. The thought of my village burning and everyone killed stopped any more protests I may have made. I told myself I could endure jail and Muneerah, even Karam, if only they were safe.

Mrs Jamal ripped off the pages she'd written on and gave me the pad and the fountain pen. She also took a bottle of ink from her briefcase.

'What else do you need? Do you have personal things with you?'

'Nahin. The police took me straight from school. I couldn't even go to my classroom to get my backpack.'

'They didn't even think to send your schoolbag along later?' She frowned.

'Mrs Jamal, it would be good to have the backpack. And a towel.'

The furrow between her eyes dug deeper into her face as she wrote notes.

'Certainly, I'll see what I can do. I'll take your glasses and have them fixed as well. Will you manage without them for a few hours?' She looked up at me and I inclined my head. I had nothing to read anyway.

'Don't send mail to your family through the post, even if they write to you. Their address will be seen. Give the letters to me and I'll send them. You can still study, so you are not behind when you are released.'

She pressed her lips together after she said 'released' and I knew she had slipped in her resolve not to lie to me.

CHAPTER

18

Karam escorted me back down the corridor but bypassed my cell and shoved me into Hafsah's cell.

'You can be a den of blasphemers and rot together.' He grinned at his joke as he slammed the door shut and locked it.

Already I hated that sound – the loud clunk as the lock turned over. This new cell was probably originally part of the one I was in first, and bars had been installed partway along to create two spaces. I could still see Kamilah and Jani as they were sitting close to the door, watching me. Kamilah handed me my mother's shawl, mat and other outfit through the bars. I gave Jani a smile, but she looked close to tears. My leaving would be a big change for a child whose world was a few metres square. This cell was smaller but at least I had a bed of my own above Hafsah's.

Hafsah said little at first and it suited me. When the azan sounded, she recited her prayers kneeling on her sleeping mat. I prayed on my mat too but we were praying with different views.

Muneerah took every opportunity to mock us. 'Once you blaspheme, God can't help you. It's unforgivable. You'll never get into heaven now.'

I didn't believe her and I hoped Hafsah didn't either. Nothing is unforgivable. It astounded me how we could worship one god and have such a different understanding of him.

'Did Muneerah beat you too?' I asked Hafsah.

She inclined her head.

'Is that why you're here by yourself?'

'I suppose. They say it's for my safety.'

'Asia Bibi is on death row in solitary confinement. I hope it doesn't get that bad for us.'

'Who is she?'

'A Masihi woman who drank from a cup Muslim women were using. They argued, then they said she blasphemed.'

Hafsah glanced at me. 'All over a cup of water?'

'Ji, like you with the quilts.'

'And you with your bad spelling.'

Then she smiled. It was the first she'd given me. 'I heard once a Muslim man and his wife were in an accident. When the motorbike was out of control it crashed into a Muslim shrine. They were both accused of blasphemy and put in jail. This is a black law.'

I sat there thinking. Abba had said that the blasphemy law was originally in place for good reasons, to protect the

146

Muslim faith in a sea of Hinduism during the Raj, but lately it was rarely used for good. Too many people used it as a weapon. And once someone was charged, even if they were proved innocent, they never seemed to lose the taint of blasphemy. It stuck like the engine grease on Abba's clothes.

'Did you come from a village?' I asked.

'Ji, it could have been a good life.' She sighed. 'But my husband's family needed sons for the farming work. Not four daughters taking everything they earn. At least she waited until I'd weaned Lala.'

My face must have crinkled up trying to understand, and she told me what had happened. 'My mother-in-law saw the quilt clipping the Qur'an. She said I did it on purpose to insult Islam.'

I was incredulous. 'Why did she say that?'

'She hates me.'

Hafsah glanced up but there was no spark of emotion in her eyes. 'I can only have girl babies. She wants a grandson, but my husband loved me – he wouldn't divorce me. So my mother-in-law arranged another marriage anyway.'

She put her arms around her legs. 'I'm glad I'm not there to see my husband marry another girl. The house is too small not to notice when he would visit her bed.'

I watched her, aghast. I even missed my little cousins, how much she must miss her own children. I didn't say what we had learned in biology: that the sex of babies is determined by the man. Miss Saima said that unless men are educated they never believe this. They only believe it if they have boys. I touched Hafsah's hand and she clasped it tight.

'I'm lucky to be alive. Some girls have acid or fire thrown at them,' she said. 'But I'll die here.'

'Surely not,' I said quickly.

She tipped her head to the side. 'It is what my husband's family wants. Even if bail was possible and they could afford it, they would never pay it. Same with Narjis.' She dipped her chin at the next cell. 'That poor woman is weak in the head. Who knows what her husband did to her. Her family won't want her now, nor will they pay bail – it's a miracle they didn't kill her.'

I didn't know what to say. How depressing. At least I knew the Colonel would have paid my bail.

That afternoon the genie brought the mail along with my glasses from Mrs Jamal. I've never known something to be fixed so quickly. No one else received a letter but there were two for me, which started Muneerah grumbling. I was glad she couldn't reach me. Both letters had no return address for the senders' safety. One was from Sammy and I retreated to my bed to read it.

Hey Cuz,

We've finally found out where you are. Dr Amal has contacted us on Facebook. I'm so sorry this has happened to you, well, to all of us actually, as we are family. We are down with Barakat's family. It's good spending time with him but I have to do my homework from school all morning. If this goes on for much

longer I may go to high school with him. He's in his last year too.
Everyone is well and we hope you are. I really hope you are okay,
Aster. It kills me that I can't do anything for you. I keep imagining
how depressing everything must be for you, and if I could swap
places I would. Never forget we love you and pray for you daily.
Everyone sends their blessings.

Your cousin, Sammy.

We love you. It brought a smile. Even though he didn't write
I love you, I knew that's what he meant. What I didn't know
is *how* he meant it. Brotherly, Masihi love or something else?
It was stupid even thinking about it. My case would probably take ages to be heard even with Mrs Jamal as a lawyer
and I'd never be let out until I was old. I was beginning to
think like Kamilah and Hafsah.

The other letter was from Afia, Barakat's sister. This one
had drawings from my little cousins. Afia's letter began
with polite protocol and it was ironic that even a letter to
me in prison could begin as if nothing had happened.

Dear Aster,

Greetings to you from Ammi and Abu and all our family.
I hope you are keeping well amidst your circumstances. I'm so
sorry that you are in prison and wrongfully so. I hope you are
getting enough to eat and that no one beats you.

People often mistreat those who they think don't matter, but
I want you to know that you matter the world to us, so please keep

*being yourself despite your trouble if you can. I can't wait until
you are returned to us.*

*I'm sewing more now and making some money from it.
Ammi has a sewing machine that works with electricity. Would
you believe we have electricity now after living here in the busti so
long without any? We even have a water pump so we don't have
to collect water with pots in the mornings. A western organisation
installed it. Maybe we can ask Uncle Yusef to buy one for your
village.*

*Noori, Akeel and Marya have each drawn you a picture on the
back and of course Rubina wanted to as well. I'm teaching the little
girls how to sew hems around dupattas, but I wish you were here to
tell them stories to keep them quiet. I don't have your talent.*

*Everyone sends their love. With all of my blessings, dear cousin,
who's like a sister.*

Afia.

I turned it over, thinking how if we'd had a water pump and
a well in the village Hadassah wouldn't have been attacked.
Akeel had drawn me with bars in front of me, angry black
bars. There were pictures of goats, butterflies and birds
from the girls but Rubina, talkative, annoying Rubina, had
drawn a heart the colours of a rainbow. It caught at me,
made me gulp down a sob.

One of the stories I had told her was about a peacock
with a tail as beautiful as a rainbow, and she had said,

A rainbow is a promise. She had made me promise to always love her.

'Aster?'

I didn't answer at first. When I looked down, little Jani almost had her face squashed between the bars, trying to see me. 'Aster, can we play?'

I took the drawings down to show her, as well as some of the paper Mrs Jamal had given me. I drew a picture for Jani and dripped blue ink out of the fountain pen to colour in the sky, then I drew a black tree from the ink bottle. It looked like a wasteland and I thought how appropriate it was for me.

Jani liked it – she'd never seen ink. 'Let me, let me,' she said.

It was obvious she'd never drawn a picture before either. She'd never seen a village, or an animal.

My eyes welled at how different her life was from that of my little cousins. Then I drew my village for her, thinking of my parents, Dadi-ji, the games we kids played, the animals, the village school, singing in church, Sammy winking at me, Hadassah's wedding.

I wondered if I'd ever experience any of it again.

CHAPTER

19

Mrs Jamal visited again. The genie took me to the inter-view room. At least I didn't have to endure Karam's innuendos. The genie stood to attention near the door, but she didn't wipe the sneer from her face quickly enough when she saw who my visitor was.

Mrs Jamal had brought my backpack with my school-books, my glasses case, and my Injeel, New Testament; also two shalwar qameezes, a blanket and a towel. Even sham-poo. When I saw the bottle I touched my hair – even in the braid it felt like wheat stalks.

I'd heard that prisoners' families should bring these things, and extra food too, but other than Mrs Jamal and Dr Amal, I had no visitors. But none of the women in my previous cell had ever had a visitor.

'How are you, Aster?' Mrs Jamal turned my face from side to side. 'No more bruises. Are you getting enough to eat?'

'Now I am.' I didn't say it was meagre compared with what we had in the village, and many times smelt off. We wouldn't grow fat like the genie in prison.

'So they put you in a single cell?'

'I'm with another girl who is accused of blasphemy.'

'Is she violent?' Mrs Jamal asked quickly.

'Nahin, just like me – she's innocent too.'

Mrs Jamal pressed her lips together. 'Her name?'

'Hafsah Ali Shah.'

She wrote it in her notebook. 'I don't remember this name. It's possible one of the other lawyers in our firm is representing her but I'll check.'

She put her pen down. 'Now, Aster,' she sat back and observed me for so long I began to worry what was wrong, 'I have seen your parents.'

I jumped off the chair. 'How are they? Are they safe?'

She nodded, then glanced at the genie. 'They are living near Rawalpindi,' she said softly.

'With my cousin Hadassah?' I whispered.

'Yes, but they cannot come to see you yet. Their names have been in the paper as parents who have reared a blasphemer. It isn't safe for them. The village has been deserted until this settles down.'

Her words were never comforting but this was terrible. Who would do the work for the landlord? Who would be working for Mrs Rafique? Would my mother ever get her job back?

'In fact,' and she licked her lips, something I'd not seen

her do, 'I've advised them to leave the country for their safety.'

'But—'

She raised her hand slightly. 'They have refused. They want to stay close to you, even though they can do nothing.'

There was silence while I digested this awful news. I didn't know whether to be sad or happy: happy that my parents loved me enough to risk their safety or sad that they were in danger.

'Now, Aster,' Mrs Jamal drew her notebook out of her briefcase and turned on the phone recorder, 'what do you think is the overriding factor of you being accused?'

I hesitated. 'Being in high school? My brother died so Abba sent me instead.'

She frowned at me. 'So you think because your brother died, you were accused?' She made it sound silly and I tried to justify myself.

'It led to it. If I wasn't in high school, I wouldn't have met Mrs Abdul—'

'Now we're getting somewhere.'

She looked up from her notebook. 'Aster, think about this carefully, do you think being a Christian was a factor?'

'I'm not sure.' I thought of Hafsah, a Muslim and still accused. Wouldn't Mrs Abdul still be angry if a Muslim girl profaned the Prophet?

'Did Mrs Abdul ever say she wanted you to become Muslim?'

'She said if I were Muslim my homework would be easier, which is true, I suppose.'

Mrs Jamal shifted on her chair.

I tried again. 'She said when I was arrested that now I'd have to become Muslim to save myself.'

'There is a school of thought that converting will lessen your punishment or at least give you a better chance to enter heaven, if you are executed.'

'I believe Khuda is bigger than—,' I stopped, suddenly realising I could have blasphemed. 'I'm sorry.'

Mrs Jamal stared at me in interest. 'You're probably right, I'm sure entering heaven has little to do with man-made laws.'

She opened her notebook to a different page. 'I have met this woman. These are the things she said about you. That you were disruptive and argumentative in class, disrespectful of her position, disrespectful of Islam by purposely not doing your homework properly, trying to convert a girl called Rabia, who, she says, confessed to this.'

She glanced up, checking my reaction. My horror must have shown, for she nodded.

'Now Aster, do you think this woman has a personal dislike of you?'

Rabia's words came back to me: *If you say the Kalimah you'll be Mrs Abdul's special project.*

I sighed. 'I felt she hated me. At first I thought it was because I was slow in her class but I grew better at my work. My friend Rabia helped me, as did Colonel Rafique, but even when I improved Mrs Abdul didn't warm to me. She only praised Rabia, not me.'

Mrs Jamal wrote a note. 'Colonel Rafique, who's he?'

'He's a family friend – actually, he's my mother's employer, but you know how it is – we have become their family.'

'I see.'

The question that was burning in me burst out of me in a panic. 'Did you believe Mrs Abdul?'

She shook her head. 'Not for a minute. Nor was I pleased when she couldn't produce the exam paper. When I said I would bring a search warrant, she said she'd burned the evil thing. Didn't want it in her classroom, nor any reminder of your perversity.'

'But now there's no proof. It's her word against mine – actually, I'm between the devil and the deep sea, aren't I? Because I don't even know what I wrote.'

'How soon after the exam did the police come?'

I groaned inside. She'd asked this before.

'We went outside to eat lunch. I didn't get to eat. It was as if the police were there immediately.'

'Immediately? Sounds premeditated to me. We know this woman destroyed the alleged blasphemous exam paper, probably because she didn't want anyone else to see it. The principal didn't see it, nor did any other senior teacher. Even the police didn't see this exam paper. A court should find that extremely interesting.'

She turned the recording off.

'This is not just because you are Christian. An elderly Ahmadi man is in prison because some college students asked him to explain his faith. They were writing a research paper. They asked to tape it so they wouldn't forget what to write. He obliged them.'

'They reported him?'

'Yes, for trying to coerce them to become Ahmadis. Even on the tape it is clear he is only explaining, not coercing, but still he is in prison.'

Mrs Jamal leaned forward. 'I am not trying to frighten you on purpose. I want to get you released. But you must realise how precarious your position is – that a woman hated you enough or believed the only way for you to become Muslim was to accuse you. Either way, she wrong-fully accused you. This is not what our constitution allows. Minority groups under the constitution are allowed to practise their own faith without persecution. Mrs Abdul persecuted you and that will be our argument.'

'Will it work, do you think?'

She raised her eyebrows. 'I will do my best.'

Then she said, 'On a happier note, there is a blog written about you.'

I lifted my head. 'Truly?'

'It's called *Free Peacock Blue*, written by a girl called Maryam Yusef Masih.' She smiled. 'My young research assistant found it. He is very thorough, and discovered this was your Facebook identity. Very sharp.'

'Maryam is my cousin, she lives in Australia.' Even I could hear the wonder in my voice. How did she do it?

'She has almost fifty thousand signatures already.'

'Signatures for what?'

'A petition. Fifty thousand people in the world believe you should be set free.'

I couldn't take it in. All those people knew about me, knew I was unjustly accused. 'From Australia?'

'From everywhere – Pakistan, the UK, America, Canada, the Middle East, Asia.'

'Can it do any good?'

She spoke as if musing. 'What will be stronger – western sentiment or the power of extremist mullahs? Hmm?'

I knew the answer to that question already – a street full of men going about their normal business could be whipped into a mob in minutes.

'It may stay a death sentence,' she said finally.

'The death sentence?' I echoed, alarmed.

She glanced at me sharply. 'Aster, you must know blasphemy incurs the death sentence.'

'Ji, I just never thought it would apply to me – I'm just a schoolkid.'

'No child has ever been given it for blasphemy.'

She sighed. 'I think your cousin's campaign can be very useful for your case. The court will not like to hear how your rights as a child are being withheld. And how the whole world knows about it.'

She put a hand over mine. 'Do not lose hope, Aster. There are people who care.'

Her words brought tears but I blinked them back quickly as she put her notebook and iPhone away.

She stood to go.

'One more thing – when you are released you need to understand you will not have your old life back. You and your parents will need to live elsewhere, probably overseas.'

I knew what she meant. Some people who didn't agree with a court's decision would take justice into their own hands.

Still, I protested, 'How can we do that? Apart from the cost, we will miss our village, our family.' Then I added softly, 'This is our country – it's all we know.'

The pity in Mrs Jamal's eyes silenced me.

'Aster, at least you will be alive – and free.'

Free Peacock Blue

To see a world where freedom,
peace and justice reign

Sign petition <u>here</u>
Target: 100,000

Rights of a Child

Bet you didn't know that in 2004 Pakistan brought back
the death penalty for children? Apparently this is because
some 17-year-olds were committing adult crimes like
murder and terrorism and needed to be controlled. The
Convention on the Rights of the Child abhors this move.
The United Nations outlines rights that children should
have, including a safe place to live, a family, education,
medical care, the right not to be bullied or hurt, the right
to say and believe what they wish, basically the right to be
themselves.

Mrs Jamal Khan, lawyer, states children in Pakistan
shouldn't be given the death penalty and holds hope that
Peacock Blue will be released. There are no reports about
her in my country but the UK papers have small pieces:
Family of schoolgirl accused of blasphemy in hiding. Village of
schoolgirl accused of blasphemy abandoned for fear of reprisals.

Please sign <u>here</u> to show your support for an innocent
schoolgirl whose rights have not been recognised and who
has been wrongfully accused. Help free Peacock Blue.

COMMENTS

Rashid I do not have the luxury to believe what suits me, to 'be myself' as you put it. You say we all have the right to be who we are, but who made up all these human rights? People in nice peaceful countries like yours, that is who, people who eat more than once a day, who have a government that gives welfare if you lose your job or your home, who do not care what you believe as long as you do not break the law. My country is a theocracy – there is no room to be myself.

Shafique My father left a country like that to keep us kids safe – he didn't agree with the majority religion.

Rashid I do not want to leave – my family are here, my roots, my ancestors – but I am always watching my back.

Sabha My Hazara father was threatened – he had to leave Afghanistan or we would have been killed. We came by boat to Australia. We had no money but the smuggler let us come for free, he understood what we were running from. It's very difficult as we didn't realise Australia does not want troubled people seeking asylum.

Asif My father was tortured in Kashmir to confess he was a terrorist. By the time the army was finished with him, he didn't even remember his name, let alone that he wasn't a terrorist. The strongest person will sign anything, especially if their family is threatened.

Maryam No one can take away what you believe inside, Rashid. Find out what that is. I find my faith keeps me stable. I'm learning happiness is a choice, whatever situation I am in.

Fozia You sound idealistic and naïve, Maryam. Maybe you look at life through the lens of your sweet country. You and me both, we can hold suffering at arm's length. When have we suffered like Asif's father or those girls abducted in Nigeria? Events like that make me see how stupid religion and talk of happiness is.

Shafique I was tortured by extremists when I was only 15 because I converted to be a follower of Christ. I survived but only because I saw a vision of Christ every time they put the electric shock on my body. I live in Canada now. But even if you haven't suffered like our family, Maryam, I still think you are right: if we give in to despair these people have won. They can hurt us physically but they can't take our soul.

Dana I don't understand how Peacock Blue blasphemed.

Fozia Do you honestly think Peacock Blue can be *happy*? Get a grip.

MESSAGES
Hadassah Bashir + 2 Salaam, cousins. Aster's parents are staying with us near 'Pindi but we're not letting them out of the walled busti (our neighbourhood) for their safety.

Maryam Yusef That's great, Hadassah. We have over 50,000 signatures on the petition already. When we get 100,000 I'll send it to the Pakistan High Commission to give to the Governor of the Punjab.

Hadassah Bashir Maybe you could send it to the lawyer who is defending her as well. The case hasn't come up yet. Sometimes it takes years, even if there is a lawyer.

Maryam Yusef Anything is worth a try. It's good she has a lawyer. Can you find her contact details? We have to get Aster out of that prison. Pity we can't break her out like Steve McQueen could.

Sammy Ibrahim She may be safer in there, have you thought of that? Barakat says hi, by the way, as does Afia and their family. We're staying with them near Lahore until this dies down, if it ever does. Maybe we should boycott the cricket – just joking.

Maryam Yusef I'll keep posting and sending the petition link via email. It's just flying around the world with this social justice website I've linked to. We have to believe that change is possible and be brave enough to say what we think. We are not attacking the country we love, we are saying that if young people like Aster are treated like this then the justice system needs reform.

CHAPTER

20

Back in the cell I unzipped my schoolbag and found the letters. The first one I opened was from Abba and Ammi. Their words showed how distraught they were. Even Abba's beautiful Urdu was uneven. They explained how it still wasn't safe for them to visit. They had to think of the whole family and community. Some of our extended family and neighbours had fled into hiding until it blew over.

Would it ever?

Even when I was released my family would have to be relocated. Abba had written me a Bible verse: *Be joyful in hope, patient in affliction, faithful in prayer.*

They loved me, exhorted me to have faith, not to lose hope. My parents' words were heartbreaking – they sounded as if they knew they had lost me forever. The blasphemy law is like a huge army tank that has no brakes. It squashes everything in its path – families, lives, hopes, dreams. I used to think of marrying one day but how could I marry anyone now? Even if I was released I'd always be the girl who was accused of blasphemy.

I opened a letter from Hadassah, also written in Urdu.

Dear Aster,

I hope you are keeping well enough in your situation. We hope and pray you will be released soon. They will have to realise what a stupid accusation this is.

I am well, and happier than I thought I'd be. Little Daud hugs me and Rebekah is growing used to me gradually – she remembers her mother more than Daud does. It is good having my family and your parents staying here but we are all sad about you. They send their love.

My husband Danyal sends his best wishes also. All the churches are praying for you. Always thinking of you, with love, Hadassah.

PS Maryam is writing a blog in English to get support for you so they will have to free you. Keep the faith.

She had included a drawing of a peacock from her step-daughter Rebekah. Hadassah must have told her I liked them. The tail feathers were pink and purple and it made me smile. At five we draw the world as we want it.

I picked through my schoolbooks and pulled out *To Kill a Mockingbird*. I didn't want to read the Islamic texts again. My parents said in their letter the school had expelled me – there was too much pressure from the other parents.

'What's that?' Hafsah said. Her voice gave me a start. She was pointing at the novel.

'It's a story we read in English class at school.'

'Can you read it?'

It was the way she said it, as though it was a tremendous feat. I answered carefully, 'Ji, just.'

'Show me.'

This was the first sign of enthusiasm I'd ever seen from her. Not that we had any reason to be enthusiastic, but she'd shown little interest at all before, even when talking about her life in the village. Maybe I'd have become like that too if I'd been here two years.

'Can you teach me to read English?'

I turned to the first page and saw the enormity of what she was asking. There was no way I could teach her to read English from the novel. I pulled out an exercise book and wrote her name in English on a page, *Hafsah*.

'See, this aitch says "huh" just like haa in Urdu.'

Her face was blank.

'Do you read often in Urdu?' I asked gently.

She shook her head. 'I had no time to learn. I was the eldest girl. I took my younger brothers to school but couldn't go myself – I had to wash their clothes, help make food.'

'How many brothers did you have?'

'Five. Aneel used to show me his homework and I began learning to read Urdu. But then he went to high school and had no time for me.'

'I can teach you to read Urdu if you like.'

'Truly?'

I smiled at the shine in her eyes.

'And you'll tell the story?' She patted the novel. 'Start that first.'

'Teik hai.'

I opened to the first page again, and silently translated each sentence before I told it in Urdu. Jani was hanging on to the bars behind me, her nose stuck between them in her effort to listen. Kamilah was probably listening as well. It was good practice for me. We had translated some parts of the story in class, but to do the whole lot would take ages and for the first time I smiled at myself. Did I have anything else to do? I'd have to censor some for Jani's ears and so I told the story. How a man, Tom Robinson, was accused of rape when he was innocent. I skipped many of the children's antics but kept some if Jani was awake.

When we reached the rape allegations in the courtroom, I was thinking of Hadassah and was startled when Kamilah gasped.

'That's what happened to me in the police station, except no one believed me.' She was outraged. 'Yet that girl was lying and everyone did believe her. That's not fair!'

It was Muneerah who asked why the story was called *To Kill a Mockingbird*. We had discussed this in class.

'Because Tom Robinson, like children or victims of prejudice, is a vulnerable person in society, just like a little bird.'

I wanted to tell the story a bit each day, so it would last longer, but Kamilah and Hafsah clamoured for it. Even Gazaalah was quiet when I spoke. It was not so strange when I remembered how much our family loved to hear stories.

The afternoon I told about Tom Robinson being killed when trying to escape, Hafsah laid a hand on my arm to stop me.

'That's what would happen to you and me if we were released.' She said it softly so no one else heard, and I shut the book without finishing the story.

The next time Mrs Jamal came she brought wool and embroidery thread for me.

'No knitting needles or crochet hooks, I'm afraid, and I had to assure that fat guard I only had one sewing needle, so don't lose it.'

She brought snacks too, including my favourite, chana. I'd be able to share it with Jani. As I reached for it Mrs Jamal took hold of my hand and turned it over.

'What's this?'

'Ink. The woman in my cell can't read or write so I teach her that in the afternoons. And I draw with Jani, a little girl. She's never drawn before.'

Mrs Jamal frowned. 'There's a child?'

I tipped my head in affirmation.

She regarded me awhile, then she said, 'You look peelah, yellow.'

It was a comment people made in my village if someone looked pale and sick.

'You need some exercise. I suppose they don't let you out in the sunshine?'

I stared at her in wonder. 'Can you do that?'

'Certainly.'

I wondered afresh at her authority. At times like this I felt safe and hopeful – maybe she would be able to have me freed. She asked me about my life in the village, what I learned at school.

'Did you study Islamiyat in the village school?'

'Ji, I know about Islam and was taught to respect it as one of the world's great religions. We studied Hinduism too. My great-grandfather was Hindu before he converted.'

'Did you learn to recite the Holy Qur'an in Arabic in the village school?'

'Nahin, but we learned what was in the Qur'an. We recited the Holy Bible instead. In Urdu.'

'Recite something for me.' She turned off the recorder.

I stood and recited my favourite scripture: chapter fourteen from Yohanna, John, about how Yesu Masih is preparing a place for us in paradise.

'Very interesting. So you can recite the whole Bible – it's very long.'

'Nahin, miss, I can tell stories from the Torah, the Old Testament, but I can only recite from the Injeel, the New Testament, and Psalms. We had tournaments. When I was twelve, I won. My cousin Sammy had always beat me but that year he went to high school.'

Mrs Jamal gazed at me a moment, her eyebrows raised. 'I'm sure it will be a consolation to you. And you speak English?'

I tipped my head again. 'It's important to learn English to study further. My brother and—' I stopped, thinking about the games we played even though we couldn't say the English 'th' or 'v'.

'Ji?' Mrs Jamal prompted.

'He spoke to me in English, for our mother didn't understand. It was like a secret language. But we learned it in the village school also. Even Colonel Rafique often spoke to me in English.'

'I suppose this Colonel Rafique would vouch for you?'

'Ji.' I thought of him storming into the police station for me.

Mrs Jamal made a few notes but I couldn't see how any of this would help show I wasn't guilty.

A few days later a new guard unlocked our cell. He was young and reminded me of Siddique.

'Out, 753!' he ordered. Hafsah grabbed my hand as if to keep me with her.

He gestured at her. 'You too.'

We didn't move quickly enough and he grabbed our arms and dragged us out. He handcuffed our wrist chains to either side of his belt and marched us down the corridor. It was hard to keep up when I'd had so little exercise.

I could hear Durrah shouting behind us, 'Your number's up, you two!'

'Good riddance, kafirs!' Muneerah added. 'They'll torture you to confess. Cut your fingers off one by one until you do.'

'Plead guilty before they start,' Gazaalah called. 'Just sign what they want, don't be a bebekoof.'

I twisted my head and saw Jani staring at us through the bars, Kamilah's face over her shoulder.

Were they right? Was I going to be tortured at last? Otherwise why bring both of us accused of the same thing?

We were marched down a different corridor where men sat in cells. When they saw us some stood and a few called out to us. The guard pushed us along but it was difficult keeping my shawl over my head with one arm. He shouted at the men but it didn't stop the heckling. We reached the end of the corridor, in front of a huge iron door.

My heart was thumping. I imagined how I'd resist converting – I couldn't betray Yesu Masih – but would I be strong enough? I'd probably sign a confession as soon as they produced a knife.

The guard unlocked the door and I shut my eyes. Hafsah gasped and my eyes flew open. We were standing in a courtyard. It wasn't big – there was just a single tree – but we were outside. *Outside.*

Even being shackled to the guard didn't dampen the joy of seeing the sky. How many weeks had it been? The leaves on the tree were still green. Still summer then. It had felt longer; I'd lost my sense of time – no school, no chores or family events to mark the passing of days. I stared upward so much I couldn't walk in a straight line and kept bumping into the officer's hip. He gave me a shove and I fell, my arm dragged upwards with a wrench. I winced.

'Can you unlock us? We can walk around the yard and not annoy you,' I said as nicely as I could manage.

'Run, not walk. I haven't time to waste on you.' But he undid the chains, and Hafsah and I linked arms and walked as briskly as we could around the little yard. And again, and yet again.

She even smiled. I was more careful; I wasn't sure if it was wise to show happiness to a guard. I imagined how the genie wouldn't think we deserved to feel joy and I had no doubt she'd smack the smile off our faces.

I could hear the traffic and when I closed my eyes I could imagine I was near the main road outside our village. All I had to do was turn around and I'd pass the wheatfields, see the buffalo turning the water wheel, the kids playing cricket, hear Sammy calling for me to join him in a game.

The genie arrived then, pulling Kamilah and Jani and two other women with children I hadn't seen before.

She saw Hafsah. 'Next time, don't bring 435 – bring this one and the child.'

Our guard had had enough. 'Ao, come.' It sounded more like 'Get over here'. Even though he was gruff I didn't mind. I hugged that thirty minutes of freedom to myself to remember later. Was this Mrs Jamal's doing? She was the real genie. What other magic did she have?

More magic happened that night. Kamilah whispered to me through the bars. I moved closer and she passed me the ear buds.

'Durrah was going to drop these down the hole but I said I wanted them.'

'You'll get in trouble with her.'

'She doesn't care about it. She just wanted to see what

you'd do. I think she was impressed that you challenged her and didn't back down.'

I squeezed her hand.

'Thank you.' I climbed to my bed with the buds in my ears, lay under the shawl and listened to Dr Amal.

Free Peacock Blue

To see a world where freedom, peace and justice reign

Sign petition <u>here</u>
Target: 100,000

Freedom of Speech – Is It Possible?

It's in our papers about an Aussie journalist being held in an Egyptian jail for what he broadcast. Does he have freedom of speech? He didn't even say what he's accused of, apparently. Is it possible to have total freedom of speech as people think of it in the west? Someone swore at me today at uni, called me a wog and said something derogatory about Islam – which would have been classed as blasphemy in a country like Pakistan or Saudi Arabia – and I'm not even Muslim. If he knew I was Christian he still would have said the same thing, just swapped the names of the prophets. So that person exercised his right to freedom of speech, but was he caring for me? Was he doing as he would like others do to him?

A program on TV recently discussed how free our speech is. They decided that what is lawful and what is acceptable can be two different things. One man said we need to stand up, speak up and say when something is not acceptable, to use free speech to help our society.

COMMENTS

Tamsin We should keep freedom of speech for the important things like abuses in politics and religion, and in our dealings with people on a daily basis we need to be polite and not offend them.

Dana You have to say what you think or you're not being honest. If my friend looks fat I tell her. She'll thank me later after she's gone on a diet.

Tamsin I pity your friends, Dana. Truth is good but truth delivered without love is judgemental and destroys relationships.

Crystal Children in the UK learn to be inoffensive through education, music and sporting activities.

Dana So what is blasphemy law anyway? Did Peacock Blue swear at the teacher?

Abdulla Thousands of people are marching saying this girl should be given the death sentence. If you don't know what blasphemy is, you all deserve what's coming to you.

CHAPTER

21

The weeks turned into two months. It was the end of July and Ramadan. Everyone fasted from sun-up to sundown; the azan, the call to prayer, told us when to pray. It was late summer, hot in the cell and no matter that I wasn't even Muslim, no food or water came until after dark. Only Jani was given a chapatti during the day.

There were no gifts for Eid ul Fitr at the end of the fast in August either. We were given chicken curry, at least, but there was so little chicken it was like Mrs Rafique's soup and didn't taste as good. Gazaalah had a set of knuckle bones and the women played together when they got too bored. It usually ended with Muneerah or Durrah shouting.

Kamilah, Jani and I relished our courtyard exercise once a week if the guards weren't too busy. Jani had been born in the cell so she often stood in awe gaping at the tree and sky. We were teased by the other women, though, when they realised we weren't being tortured.

A few days after Eid a small parcel came. The genie seemed hesitant to give it to me. It had been opened and checked. By her? If so, it had to be something she didn't care for. Dr Amal had sent me batteries for the Walkman but they were confiscated; when I received that envelope only the note remained.

This parcel was from Sammy. There was a note, but no return address as usual.

Hey Cuz,

I thought I'd send these as everyone else might be getting gifts from their families for Eid and you'd be the odd one out. We miss you and hope you are okay.

All our love, Sammy.

Inside were twelve tiny tubes of paint and two paintbrushes in a tin. His thoughtfulness brought me to tears. He was looking after me like a brother. What would Ijaz had done if he was alive? But I was glad he never saw me like this. Ijaz didn't have Sammy's lightness; he would have gone mad not being able to save me.

I thought of the good times. The harvesting that we all helped with. The village school was shut on harvest days so we helped the men with the winnowers like huge flour sieves, as they tossed the grain high, separating the chaff from the grain. We had a harvest festival in church when it was all finished and thanked Khuda for his kindness and grace. Even though it was the landlord's land we received a percentage.

I took out one of my exercise books and drew pictures of the harvest with a peacock in the foreground. Before Sammy sent the paints I only had ink to paint with and I used my finger or a piece of paper. I had missed colours so much – there was no peacock blue in the cell. It was the first colour I used.

Jani watched me. 'Can I do that too?'

I shifted closer to the bars dividing us, handed her a brush and ripped a piece of paper out for her.

'What will you paint?' I asked.

'A bird like yours.' Jani had never seen a peacock or a cow or a goat. Not even a chicken, so I drew them for her. I drew our whole courtyard for her to colour in.

When letters or parcels came I felt better, even if the genie or Karam threw them in and they landed in the muck on the floor. The cleaner didn't come every day, and we had no way to wash the cell ourselves.

Some days I was scared and cowered on my bed, not able to move. I felt I was standing at the entrance to a tunnel in a cornfield in early summer, knowing I would have to walk through it alone and the cobras were waking. Sometimes Hafsah was feeling low and sometimes me, but never usually at the same time, so we could pull each other out of bed before a guard came with breakfast. The genie was the strictest about being out of bed. The food smelt – I felt ill most of the time. Sometimes I couldn't wait to get to the toilet in the mornings and had to relieve myself over the hole. I washed water down, embarrassed about the smell.

A letter came from Hadassah.

Piari Aster

Greetings from us all in Rawalpindi. I hope you are managing to bear up under your extreme suffering. A verse that helped me last year was 'Wait on the Lord; be of good courage, and he will strengthen your heart.'

I pray for you all the time, for in one way we have a similar path: you are accused wrongly and I would have been too if anyone had known. Little Daud calls me Ammi, even Rebekah forgot her reticence a few weeks ago when she had a bad dream and cried for me to come. She is polite with me now.

My life is fine after the harrowing experience I've had, and I pray yours will be so when you are released. It will be a different life than you imagine perhaps, but Khuda is with us wherever we are – in the belly of a fish, or in the cell of a prison.

Please don't lose hope or faith. I couldn't bear it if you lost yourself. Your father is working as a rickshaw driver and does tailoring too so your parents are fine, though they worry about you. Everyone misses you so much and sends love. All my love, dear sister-cousin,

Hadassah Bashir.

The genie threw a paper into our cell as she delivered the breakfast next morning. 'Read that and see what happens to evil girls like you.'

There was a picture of a girl my age. *A Light in the Dark,* the title read. I read the article to Hafsah.

We strongly condemn the attack on Malala Yousafzai and her friends. Members of the Taliban studied the daily route that Malala took to school in Swat when girls were being discouraged against going to school. But Malala stood up for girls' right to an education. When they shot her the Taliban took responsibility, saying she had spoken against them.

The poor girl, I knew what it felt like to be falsely accused. 'They vow to shoot her again if she survives.'

'Where is she now?' Hafsah asked.

I scanned the article. 'This happened a while ago. It must be the anniversary. Now she's in England, in a town called Birmingham.'

'I hope she stays there and makes a life for herself.'

Malala sounded like the sort of person who would want to come back and finish what she started. If she wasn't so young, what a prime minister she would make. But it was a dangerous job. Anything was, when you stood up for someone else. Salman Taseer was murdered after he supported Asia Bibi and others like her on death row.

'What else does it say?'

'That we need critical thinking in education—'

'What's that?' Kamilah asked.

Surprisingly Muneerah answered, 'It means being able to think for yourself and not just believe the crap we get fed.'

I kept reading. *It has the power to diffuse terrorism. It is an internal liberation that jihadism cannot offer. Malala said before she was shot that if the new generation is not given pens they will be given guns by the terrorists. We must raise our voice.*

I stopped. I'd just realised that Malala was Gul Makai. She'd been writing in the papers under that assumed name years ago. I looked for the author of the article and found with a shock that it was the daughter of Salman Taseer, the assassinated governor of the Punjab who believed in social justice and reforming the blasphemy law.

I couldn't read any more and put the paper down. I was sure the genie hoped to demoralise me, but reading about Malala from the courageous daughter of such a brave man was like putting a match under a dying fire. A phrase that I hadn't read aloud from the article kept reverberating in my mind: *the power of ignorance is frightening*.

But what could I do in prison to help my situation – or anyone else's who was in the same predicament?

The women in the next cell were quiet for a long time after I read from the article. Then Muneerah said, 'They shouldn't have shot her – she was just a good girl who could think for herself.'

'What's wrong with girls being educated anyway?' Kamilah asked.

Most of the women glanced my way but Gazaalah observed me with a frown.

'Nothing,' she said, 'as long as they still obey their parents and do the right thing.'

She lifted her chin at me through the bars. 'You, poor thing, couldn't help being born a Masihi, I suppose.'

I didn't feel like explaining that we aren't born into faith. We accept Khuda's invitation to believe and if we decide not to, our parents don't beat us. Our faith is in Khuda's hands, not theirs.

Muneerah let loose a snort. 'Men don't like educated girls because we get ideas of our own. They want us to be mindless slaves, still living in the dark ages, to bring up boys who treat women just like we have been.'

The bitterness squirted out of her like a lanced boil. I stared at her until I checked myself and looked back at the paper, but I couldn't see the words – they were too blurred.

Later, after her sleep, Jani wanted a story.

'Tell me your favourite one,' she asked.

I tried not to mind, even though I felt tired. Jani had helped me more than I'd known at first. Without her would I still be able to think, to remember things? Would I be like Hafsah when I first went into her cell – not caring or remembering, just sleeping all day?

In the village I used to tell the story of Queen Aster's choosing and wedding. It was every girl's dream, and mine. But the wedding wasn't the end of the story. There was intrigue, injustice, racism and ethnic cleansing.

'Would you like one about a queen in Persia a long time ago?'

Jani's eyes brightened a little. It would be lovely to see what she would be like living free in a village like Sammy's little sisters, Marya and Noori. When I told them the story of Aster, they were so full of happy questions.

I began, 'Once there was a queen in Persia called Aster.'

'Like you?' She looked surprised. 'You're not a queen. You're a prisoner like Ammi.'

I swallowed. I still couldn't get used to being called a prisoner. I carried on with the story. 'Queen Aster was a Jew but no one knew.'

'What's a Jew?'

'It's a religion but it's not Muslim.'

'Like you? You're not Muslim.'

She probably had never heard of another faith.

'Nay, I'm Masihi, not Jewish either.' I continued, 'Her guardian, Mordecai, heard about a terrorist plot that two officials were planning against the king and he told Aster to warn him. The plot was uncovered and the officials were hanged. The king ordered Mordecai's name to be recorded so he could be rewarded. Next, the king appointed an advisor called Haman. He was proud and not nice at all.'

'Like Green Eyes?'

'Maybe. Haman hated Mordecai because he wouldn't bow to him. He wanted revenge so he deceived the king to have every Jew murdered, which would include Mordecai.'

'He's mean.'

'Ji, and so Mordecai told Aster about it. "You have to ask the king to stop it."

'"How can I do that? I have to be invited to see the king. If I approach him and he is displeased he will have me killed."

"'Do you know how many people will suffer? Hundreds of thousands of people living in the provinces from India to Africa will be slaughtered and you cannot escape either. Are you not Jewish?"

'Queen Aster said, "Pray for me and fast for three days. Then I will go to the king, even though it is against the law. And if I perish, I perish."'

I paused – could I do something like that? She wouldn't have been able to live with herself afterwards if she hadn't tried.

'After three days, Queen Aster put on her purple royal robes and stood in the inner court of the palace. The king was struck anew at her beauty and he held out his sceptre. She walked towards him and touched it.

"'What is it?" he asked. "Whatever you ask for, I will give it."

"'If it pleases my Lord," she said, "come with Haman to a banquet I have prepared." The king was so intrigued he immediately called for Haman and they went to her rooms. After they had eaten the king asked again. "Tell me what it is you would like and I will give it, even half the kingdom."

"'Nay, I ask only for my life and that of my people and Mordecai. We are to be annihilated. Please spare us, we are Jews and we are innocent."

'Then the king remembered how Mordecai had saved him from the terrorist plot. "Who would plan to kill Mordecai? And you?"

"'It is this man, Haman, my Lord."

'The king was so angry that he ordered Haman to be hanged on the gallows he'd built for Mordecai. Then he chose Mordecai as his advisor and, since a royal decree couldn't be revoked, an order was sent out to the provinces that on the day the Jews would be attacked they were allowed to fight back. It became the day of Pur, a time in years to come for feasting, as Jews remembered the victory over the people who hated them just because they were Jews.'

I heard Muneerah mumbling, 'Those Jews, bombing our people, deserve everything they get.'

'That's a sad story,' Jani said.

'Why? Queen Aster saved her people. She's a superhero.'

'But no one will save you. Muneerah says you will hang.'

Kamilah tried to shush her and I was so shocked, I turned abruptly to face the other way.

Kamilah whispered behind me, 'Don't take any notice. They wouldn't hang a girl like you. No one has been executed for blasphemy, not even those who have been given the death sentence. Aster?'

I didn't answer. Asia Bibi was given the death sentence, and yes, she was still alive, but living on death row would be an end to life whether you were executed or not.

Free Peacock Blue

*To see a world where freedom,
peace and justice reign*

Sign petition <u>here</u>
Target: 125,000

Blasphemy Law

Dana asked in a post what blasphemy is. In a country
like mine it's not something we think about, so here is
my research about blasphemy law. Wiki says blasphemy
law is one that limits freedom of speech and expression
relating to blasphemy or irreverence towards a religion.
Australia's constitution prohibits a state religion so it
hasn't prosecuted anyone for blasphemy since 1919, but
hate speech, i.e. speech that attacks a person or group
on the basis of race, religion, gender, disability or sexual
orientation, is not tolerated. People who feel they have
been vilified according to their religion could seek redress
under legislation that prohibits hate speech.

In the UK the last person to be executed for blasphemy
was in the seventeenth century, though a film was banned
for blasphemy in 1989. In most countries blasphemy is
not a crime, though in Spain people can be prosecuted for
vilifying religious feelings and dogmas.

Pakistan is not the only country with a current
blasphemy law. (I counted at least a dozen, though there
are more, and some like Ireland only have a fine and
Norway hasn't used theirs for 80 years.) Blasphemy is a

serious matter in Pakistan as well as in Afghanistan and many other countries with Sharia law (which can demand the death sentence for blasphemy); no one is to disrespect the Prophet Muhammad or Islam.

However, the sad thing is, the blasphemy law in some countries, including Pakistan, is often used as a weapon or in a personal vendetta. People are discriminated against even if they are only charged. Even if the court says they are innocent, they are not safe once they are released. So how will Peacock Blue fare? When she is released she will need to be relocated to a country that doesn't observe blasphemy law.

COMMENTS

Rashid My country has just passed a law that Muslims who change their religion must be given the death sentence. They call changing your religion from Islam blasphemy.

Habib People should be punished for disrespect of the Qur'an and our Prophet.

Fozia If Muhammad's name can't be disrespected does that mean Eid cards can't be thrown in the bin? Newspapers with the name Muhammad in them can't be thrown away or burned to get a fire started. How many million people have the name Muhammad? This is ridiculous.

Amir A man was sentenced to death recently for defiling the name of the Holy Prophet. A 3000-strong mob attacked his neighbourhood, leaving hundreds of people homeless. It was motivated by a property dispute between him and his friend.

Ahmed In our paper a couple was accused of sending blasphemous text messages. The texts came from the wife's mobile phone which she'd lost and the lawyer discovered neither of them could write Urdu well enough to even send a text. Still, the husband was tortured and they were both given the death sentence. The judge must have been intimidated by the prosecution lawyer.

Affat This year one of our newspapers conducted a poll and found that 68% of Pakistanis believe the blasphemy law should be repealed.

Dana This whole discussion is disgusting. What if people like that come to Australia and want their laws here? We'll all get our hands chopped off and be murdered in our beds.

Maryam What we need is a greater awareness of the lives of others, to release us from self-absorption and help us to understand.

CHAPTER

~≈~

22

Men in black rush to burn the village. They see me and drag me with them. I am the only one left alive and I scream as they push me into a cage on wheels to take me away. They chant as if they are part of a drama, 'We will hang you, hang you, hang you!'

The dreams didn't leave me alone, yet I knew there was nothing I could do about them. Hafsah showed me this. All the women, even Muneerah, had a kind of silent despair clinging to them and the longer they'd been in prison the more resigned they became. They didn't 'wait' for anything as there was nothing to wait for.

At least I had Mrs Jamal. She and my faith helped me get up each morning. And now I had Malala to think about. I kept the article about her, and the creases became worn from reading it so many times. Malala stood up to the Taliban because she knew girls should be free to go to school, whatever anyone said. I knew I should also be free to have my own faith.

But I wasn't like Malala. Sammy called me loud, and I could sing in front of a congregation, but I didn't feel confident anymore.

Could I do what Malala did? Not the girl I was becoming.

One good thing came from having the article. I started a calendar in an exercise book and crossed off each day. Hafsah said it would make me go mad, but I didn't agree. It was autumn – the tree in the courtyard had lost its leaves.

Hafsah told me about Muneerah one night. 'She had a secret love marriage, for she knew her parents wouldn't accept the boy she loved. When she fell pregnant her father had her arrested for zina. The family didn't recognise the marriage and one of her uncles killed her young husband. When she had the baby in here last year the family took him away.'

I could hear the screams in my head as Hafsah said softly, 'She doesn't know if they killed him or let him live. It's unhinged her, like Narjis, just in a different way. Everyone goes mad in here sooner or later.'

No wonder Muneerah had no visitors. Her family thought of her as dead.

The weather grew colder. Bara Din, Christmas Day, was coming. Cards with drawings came from my little cousins. I had no envelopes but I wrote letters back for Mrs Jamal to send.

My parents sent me a new shalwar qameez through Mrs Jamal. It looked like one of Juli Rafique's, for it was made of woollen cloth. It was good I was in a cell with Hafsah and we went to the washroom at a different time from the next cell, or I might not have been able to keep the outfit from Durrah. I saw her eyes gleam through the bars as I drew it from the package.

Finally Mrs Jamal told me my court case would be heard in a week's time. On the day, I carefully washed and dressed in the woollen outfit. I plaited my hair three times to get it neat and sat in Ammi's warm shawl until the genie came to take me to the police van. If they found me innocent, surely I wouldn't be returning, so I had the fountain pen and Sammy's letters in my pocket.

'Don't know why you're all dressed up,' the genie sneered. 'You'll be back soon.'

I tried not to show how her words affected me.

Police officers guarded me as we went in the back door of the courthouse. Mrs Jamal was already there.

'We'll wait here,' she said crisply. 'The case before us is taking a long time.'

We went over the questions that would be asked.

'Remember, you won't speak,' she said.

I nodded nervously. Would they decide I was innocent? What if someone outside decided I was guilty?

Mrs Jamal looked at her watch and disappeared into another room, her high heels tapping. Two guards stayed with me but they said nothing. Mrs Jamal brought back two cups of tea and biscuits. We each had one biscuit and then I ate the rest of them. I hadn't seen one in the six months I'd been in jail. I felt guilty but Mrs Jamal was distracted and didn't seem to notice.

A court official called to her from the door. When she returned she was angry. 'They miscalculated the time. Your case won't be heard today after all.' Her voice softened when she saw my face. 'I'm very sorry, but sometimes this happens.'

I cried in the van on the way back to the prison. In a little corner of my mind I had hoped I'd be freed and I wouldn't need to return, that my parents would be there to receive me and we'd all live with Hadassah.

'So you didn't get heard,' Gazaalah said as I was let into my cell. She didn't sound sorry about it, as if she'd known all the time. I ignored her and Hafsah left me alone to lie on my bed.

Dr Amal came the next day. I didn't know if he was in contact with Mrs Jamal but his timing was perfect. And he had batteries for me.

'How did you know the ones you sent went missing?' I asked.

'I didn't. But my mother told me it was stupid to send things like that through the mail.'

'Why do they get confiscated?'

'There must be a list of things you're not supposed to have, or maybe the officer checking the mail that day needed some.'

I imagined the genie taking them. I couldn't seem to

manage a smile and there was silence. I hoped he wouldn't ask how I was, for I knew I'd weep.

So before he could speak I said, 'My court hearing has been postponed.'

I said it firmly and he nodded at me.

'It happens a lot,' he said. 'Some people wait years. Asia Bibi's appeal to the High Court has also been postponed again.'

Tears sprang to my eyes. I knew there were many worse off than me, but still I'd hoped.

'There are many people praying for you, Aster, even outside of Pakistan.'

I glanced up at him and tried to smile.

'I have written a song for you.'

Now that was surprising. 'Truly?'

He tilted his head. 'I was thinking of Job and Hannah in the Bible, how the fulfilment of their hope was delayed. Then I thought of you.'

His eyes were full of empathy. Not pity, at least, even though he must have known I may never get out of prison. It was what I tried not to think about.

'It's about waiting for the Lord, however long it takes. Even if we are in the next world before our hope is realised, he will be faithful.'

Looking at him I realised something: I did want God to get me out of here. Isn't that what hope is? Wanting something good to happen? Or is hope giving up the right to have things the way we want and letting God do what he thinks best?

If I asked Hafsah she'd say he wasn't interested in us.

I existed from day to day, night to night. Weeks became months, and I wondered why it was so difficult to get another hearing in court. Did they make us wait on purpose? Or were there too many cases and not enough judges?

Finally in late February it was time to get ready for court again. This time Mrs Jamal hopped from heel to toe in the waiting room. When she was called to the corridor like last time, she frowned. I watched her back as she spoke with a person, then returned to me.

I held my breath, then asked, 'What is it?'

'Your teacher hasn't turned up.'

'Mrs Abdul?' I said in sudden hope. 'Has she changed her mind? Will she withdraw the accusation?'

Mrs Jamal shook her head. 'It's too late for that – the damage has been done. No, this is called mind games, or maybe she's stubbed her toe.'

I stared at her, appalled. 'She just didn't arrive? No reason?'

'No reason. I'm sorry, Aster. It's been postponed until next month.'

I couldn't help the tears. That was what they'd said last time but it had taken more than one month. And then what? The lawyer mightn't turn up. The judge might have a bilious attack, all while I waited and waited and waited. In prison.

Back in the cell I took the article about Malala from under my blanket. She wouldn't give up. Even in Britain she was gaining an education and doing speeches. She must be waiting for when she could return. In a way she was in captivity too, in exile. I prayed for strength like hers to endure the waiting.

Dreams were with me constantly but they'd changed. Now they weren't all bad. They were a place where I could disappear, to be happier. I dreamed I was in a boat. At first the waves were gentle. Fish jumped over the waves. One landed in the boat. Then the waves rose higher until the boat was as high as a mountain and I knew it would crash. I screamed and suddenly someone appeared in the boat with me. He used a pole and the boat didn't capsize as we rode down the wave with white curling foam circling us. I saw his face before the next wave came. He was enjoying the exhilaration of the ride. It was Yesu Masih. I was not alone.

When I woke I tried to catch the feeling of joy the dream had given me, but it slipped like sand through my fingers. I wished I was still asleep. After breakfast the genie came to get me.

'Visitors for you.' She sounded annoyed, as if I was receiving too many privileges. She chained me as usual and escorted me to the interview room. With my meagre exercise I didn't walk as well as I used to and she pulled me down the last corridor. She had no time to move slower for me.

I saw Mrs Jamal first and there were two other people. One was a woman in a burqa, but something about the way she stood was familiar. I hardly dared hope as they turned around. The lady lifted the burqa veil.

I gave a gasp and fell into Ammi's arms. I thought I'd be happy, I'd dreamed of this moment, but I couldn't stop the sobs. I sensed Abba standing beside me, before he put his arms around both of us. He prayed for me to be released, and gave thanks for our family, our love, and it calmed me a little.

'We've wanted to come,' Ammi said, 'but it's been too dangerous on the bus. Mrs Jamal brought us in her car.'

No doubt that was why she was wearing the burqa; she'd never worn one before.

I drank them in, looking at one and then the other, in between my tears.

'You've lost so much weight,' my mother said before she could stop herself. 'Good thing we brought food for you.'

'I'm sorry I've caused so much trouble, for you, the village . . .' I wanted them to take me now, back home to my old life.

'What if they find me guilty? I can't do this without you,' I gabbled, 'not without Sammy, Hadassah, Ijaz . . .' My voice trailed away as Abba took my face between his hands.

'Aster,' he murmured, 'my beautiful beti, it is not your fault. What makes our life different wherever we are, even in a prison, is the presence of Khuda and his love. He is in control whether we feel it or not. Just trust him and he will help you persevere. Then hope will come.'

His eyes teared up and I knew he wanted to grab me and take me home. He hugged me to himself so tightly I could hardly breathe.

'My beti—' His voice broke and Ammi took me from him.

'Chup, chup, quiet,' she said like she had when I couldn't sleep at night as a little child.

She didn't say everything would be fine, she just swayed me from side to side like a baby.

'I'm sorry your case hasn't been heard but we hope it happens soon. They will see you are a good girl.'

I hoped she was right.

Then she said, 'Love is stronger than death, Aster.'

She stood back to look at me and I saw in her face the effort she made to be strong for me.

'We have a gift from Hadassah.'

It was a cushion, and embroidered on it was my painting of the peacock that I'd put on my Facebook page. My eyes watered. It was a reminder I was cared for and not to give up, a reminder of my real life and of Maryam's blog.

My parents gave me a book of promises for my birthday. We never made much of birthdays in the village, but I would be fifteen soon. Inside was fifty rupees in ten-rupee notes.

'You may need that,' Abba said when he saw my surprise. 'Keep it hidden and remember to read the Holy Word and it will comfort you. Everyone is praying.'

We all knew prayers weren't always answered the way we think they will be. What if Khuda allowed me to stay in here like Job, who had to go through his suffering? Yusef was in prison for years before he became the governor of Egypt. But Danyal was saved from the lion's den.

Would I be too?

CHAPTER

23

Time had travelled slower through the winter and early spring. Seeing my parents helped me settle more but at times I didn't hear Hafsah when she spoke. Some days she didn't hear me either. There were days I felt I was standing on the edge of a roof and I became dizzy, like I'd fall.

Little Jani could pull me back. 'Tell me a story, Aster.' Or 'Draw with me, Aster.'

I did things mechanically – I drew through the bars or held her hand as I told a story. Often I forgot where I was up to, and she prompted me. I caught Kamilah watching me with a worried frown. I thought of Abba and tried to hold all of me together, I didn't want any pieces slipping away, I didn't want to be like Narjis.

Why was waiting so hard?

Finally, at the end of March not long after Pakistan Day, when the leaves had begun growing on the courtyard tree, the time came. I hoped that this was the day and I wouldn't have to return again, without knowing what my fate would be.

Mrs Jamal had said to dress as a schoolgirl this time, so I dressed carefully in my school uniform. It was a year since I had dressed as carefully as this when I began high school.

Ammi was right, the uniform was loose on me, and I could feel my hipbones through my shalwar. I plaited my hair, placed my scarf on my head and covered myself with the shawl. I was nervous, but also tired of not knowing my fate. Wouldn't knowing be better than this feeling of an impending monsoon that never gave rain?

Hafsah didn't know what would happen to her and it made her listless. When someone remembered she was here, would they finally hear her case? If it weren't for Mrs Jamal I'd be in the same situation.

Again, I was taken in a black police van, handcuffed to an officer. I was whisked into the building under my shawl through a back door with riot police standing guard. Yet again we waited in a small room and I thought, *This is going to be the same. How many times will I be brought and nothing will happen?*

After two hours Mrs Jamal met with me. 'I've changed my mind about you not speaking,' she said. 'With the Colonel as a witness, the judge may feel sympathy for your plight. Keep it short, just say how old you are, what it's like in prison as a child. And most importantly, that you are innocent of the charge. You won't be cross-examined – they would make you blaspheme just by asking you a simple question about your faith.'

I must have looked as panicked as I felt, for she said, 'There will be time to get it straight in your head. The case being heard is taking longer again, but I have been assured your case will be heard this afternoon.'

The waiting was even worse than in the prison. What if I get sent back again?

But Mrs Jamal was right. After a few more hours we were called to the courtroom, which gave me confidence that she would be right about the defence as well. She was my Atticus Finch.

The court was already filled with people when we entered. I saw a bench up the front, the judge with a gold sash around his neck. I bowed my head in his direction as I entered. I had to stand chained to two officers on either side of me. Mrs Jamal sat at a table in front of us. Her assistant turned to give me a smile, but my mouth wouldn't work to return it.

The other lawyer walked in and Mrs Jamal exclaimed. She and her assistant exchanged words. Something was wrong and she glanced worriedly at me. She stood and asked to approach the bench but the judge refused, and ordered her to begin.

She called her best witness to the stand, Colonel Rafique. He was a character witness to show I would never have intentionally blasphemed. He said I was a good girl and studied hard. There was more I couldn't remember later. The prosecutor questioned him then.

'Colonel Rafique Ali Khan, you've known this girl, Aster

Suleiman Masih, all her life, I understand.' The lawyer drew out my family name slowly for the court to digest.

'That is correct.'

'You are Muslim?'

'Certainly.'

'But she is not. Why haven't you shown her the true path?'

The Colonel frowned. 'Your questioning isn't in line with the case.'

The lawyer looked down his multifocal glasses at the Colonel. 'Let the court decide what is in line, Colonel.'

I could see what the lawyer was doing and it made me feel tired. There was no way the Colonel could answer to please them unless he made it worse for me.

'Sustained,' the judge said.

'Answer the question.' The lawyer stared at the Colonel.

'If God wanted her to change religions he would have put it in her heart to do so.' Then he said, 'You are an educated man, why are you taking this ridiculous stance? Look at that girl,' and he pointed at me. 'You can see she's innocent.'

'Education of your sort draws people away from God.'

'I haven't left the faith even though I'm educated.'

'That is not the evidence I have before me.'

The Colonel thumped the stand. 'How dare you make a subjective judgement about my faith? This is outrageous, it's nothing short of an inquisition.'

The judge called him to order and more was said to goad the Colonel to put me in a bad light. Tears ran down my face and I closed my eyes; I couldn't bear to see him so humiliated.

Anyone else would have said, 'Yes, I tried to convert her but she didn't listen' to show how deserving of the sentence I was, but the Colonel wouldn't give them that satisfaction.

Mrs Abdul did. 'Time and time again in class this apostate had chances to join the true faith, but she stubbornly refused, clinging to her idol worship of three gods.'

It was Rabia, poor Rabia who tried to convert me, and it wasn't even for my spiritual welfare.

Mrs Jamal took Mrs Abdul to task over the missing exam and why she didn't show it to anyone else. Her argument should have worked, but Mrs Abdul appealed to the judge and a line of bearded clerics in dark shalwar qameezes in the front row.

'Your worship, I had to do my duty, I couldn't bear the evil thing in my classroom. It would taint the other girls. I burned it immediately.'

The judge glanced at the clerics and they all dipped their heads like crows around a carcass. He asked Mrs Jamal to take another line of questioning.

She shifted her notes. 'Under our constitution minority faiths are allowed to practise their religion and are not to be persecuted. Mrs Abdul, you have broken that law by your own admission in trying to force Aster Suleiman Masih to become Muslim.'

'I wanted the best for her. I didn't want her to burn in hell.'

I'd never heard her speak so sweetly, like almond halva. She sounded like the ideal teacher with all her students' needs in mind, and the clerics' crow heads bobbed in time again.

'Do you deny beating Aster?'

'No, I had to discipline her often – she was very disruptive in class.'

'We only have your word on this.'

Mrs Abdul drew herself up and a look came over her face that belonged to the Mrs Abdul I knew. 'My word should be enough for anyone who is a true Muslim.'

Mrs Jamal called for another witness. Miss Saed-Ulla, wearing a shawl over her head, was brought to the stand by a man who must have been her father. She didn't mind saying what she thought of Mrs Abdul.

She indicated the line of clerics in the front row. 'Her brother is a mullah at the local mosque and he has probably advised her on how to deal with the "only Christian girl" in class. Treatment like this of such students must stop. Mrs Abdul targeted Aster because she was Christian, she said so in the staffroom one day. "I will beat that kafir religion out of her," she said. "You'll see, by the end of first term she'll be Muslim." It was as if it was her project to convert Aster.'

This sounded helpful but by the time the prosecution was finished with Miss Saed-Ulla, Mrs Abdul looked like a saint. The lawyer had discovered Miss Saed-Ulla taught western novels in English classes. I thought lawyers were educated – surely he'd read western books? Why were they suddenly bad, and why did it seem like he was building a case against educating girls?

Mrs Jamal didn't receive the respect that I thought she deserved. It was like a fantastical story Ijaz told me once about a girl called Alice, whose court case was run by the Queen of Hearts. Except for Mrs Jamal, the Colonel and Miss Saed-Ulla, this whole court was a façade, just like a pack of cards that could be blown away.

It was my turn to speak. Mrs Jamal was frowning as I was asked by the judge what I pleaded. My tongue felt stuck to the roof of my mouth. Even the other lawyer looked impatient and annoyed.

'Not guilty,' I finally said. 'I would never have intentionally blasphemed. I don't know what I wrote that could be so bad, my teacher didn't tell me. I was accused when I was fourteen and it has been difficult in jail as a schoolgirl, but I believe Khuda will help me.'

I couldn't think of anything else. There was no pity on anyone's face except the Colonel's and Miss Saed-Ulla's. The clerics had looked pleased when I said it was difficult in jail.

Mrs Jamal stood. 'There is no evidence whatsoever that Aster Suleiman blasphemed. Everyone except Mrs Abdul says she is a respectful and intelligent girl who cares for others, who has Muslim friends as well as Christian ones. There is only one person's word standing between this child and freedom.'

I felt strange, as if I was kneeling on a cloud and could see a bright light, like Stephen did when he was being stoned for blasphemy. The cloud disappeared and I was left staring at the floor.

I could hear the judge pronouncing me wilful and guilty, then sentencing me to death. I grabbed hold of the chair in front of me so I wouldn't fall against the policemen. My chest heaved; I couldn't control the sobs.

Mrs Jamal shouted that a Pakistani court shouldn't give the death sentence to a child – what was the judge doing, bowing to uneducated religious leaders who weren't following the true Islam? 'We're being led into the dark ages.'

The Colonel tried to calm her. He was weeping, then he hugged me.

Mrs Jamal shuffled her notes together and actually put an arm around me.

'I'm sorry, Aster,' she said. 'We proved it was just one woman's vindictiveness but the court's been rigged. The lawyer was switched at the last minute – this man has a history of taking blasphemy cases and winning – they've threatened the judge or bribed him, I'm sure of it. I'm sorry, it's been a circus, but we'll appeal to the High Court and if they also agree with the verdict, we'll go to the Supreme Court.'

I wept into her shoulder. None of my family was there – it would have been too dangerous. As it was there were many policemen, not only guarding Mrs Jamal and me and her witnesses, but to contain the crowd. The police I was chained to were pulling on my arms.

'We have to take her now, madam,' one said to Mrs Jamal. 'You too, quickly.'

The other policeman leaned closer to me. 'No need to weep,' he said. 'The sentence will keep you safe.'

I glanced up, sniffing. He had skin like mine and looked as if he would cry himself.

'I'll see you soon,' Mrs Jamal said, when we reached the back door. 'Don't give up hope.'

I could hear shouts from outside, cheers. 'Let's kill her now – save the government some rope!'

More clerics were outside and there was so much shouting it sounded like the end of Ramadan, as if the people had much to celebrate. Men were even dancing in the street. How did they find out I was inside? I hoped they wouldn't stone me. Shooting or even hanging would be quicker. If I had said the Kalimah I may have been saved, but Mrs Jamal had said I shouldn't have to, and I agreed. Did she ever imagine she would lose?

Lines of riot police and soldiers in khaki with helmets and guns lined the street, trying to keep the mob away from the courthouse as courthouses have been attacked before. Other police officers had shields and two accompanied us, one in front and one behind, as we got in the van. There was a shot but I didn't see if anyone fell. I was pushed in and landed on the floor with the two officers. Our legs were entangled and I managed to get mine to myself. The two men with the shields jumped in too. I glanced up at the officer who had told me not to weep and as he shifted to get more comfortable I saw the glint of a chain at his neck. There were thumps on the outside of the van, shouts to give up their vile cargo.

'Do not worry,' the darker-skinned officer said, 'the van is bulletproof.' What if they bombed it? I would be like Tom Robinson. I could see the headline: *Schoolgirl shot while escaping*.

The policeman added, 'It is little Eid. It is when hope begins.'

I stared at him. He was saying it was the Easter festival. I didn't know, since it's a different date each year. Yesu Masih was given the death sentence for blasphemy at the first Easter. I was His follower – why should I expect any less?

Yet still I prayed my sentence could be revoked. *I am not Khuda, I am just a girl.*

I wanted to return home and our lives to be the same again. I'd never disobey my parents or disappear when there were chores to do. *But I am fooling myself – my life will never be the same.* If I were to be released I'd have to flee the country and become an asylum seeker. Would my parents come too? Would we live with Maryam's family in Australia? Like Malala Yousafzai who was still in Britain. Would she ever be able to come home?

I couldn't talk about it in the cell. I was frozen. Hafsah knew I had been given the death sentence. I bet the genie told them. With glee.

'I'm sorry,' Hafsah said.

I kept thinking, if the Colonel had said this or Mrs Jamal had said that, but always I came back to the same conclusion: whatever was said, the prosecution would have turned it over like a shovel mucking out a goats' pen.

Mrs Jamal was right: the court had been tampered with. It had felt like a lion's den and I hadn't been delivered.

That night I dreamed I was in the courtyard. A light shone and grew closer and there was Yesu Masih, holding out His hand. He wore a long cream robe and a shawl that was so bright it made the whole land shine with colour. He looked as strong as if He could overthrow a court or a whole government if He wished it, but it was me He wanted. His dark eyes brimmed with compassion.

'Beloved Aster.' His voice reverberated in the sky and His love settled around me like a blanket made of peacock feathers.

Such power and light I had never experienced. I knew then Yesu had delivered me, just in a different way from what I'd expected, deep inside me, for when I woke I was not so afraid.

Free Peacock Blue

*To see a world where freedom,
peace and justice reign*

Sign petition <u>here</u>
Target: 200,000

Freedom of Religion – Is there such a thing?

We are all supposed to enjoy the right to freedom of
religion but today I can't think of what to say about it. My
fifteen-year-old cousin Peacock Blue has just been given
the death sentence because she's the wrong religion.

There was no jury, as juries in multicultural countries
with ethnic tensions can be biased. India and Pakistan
abolished the system soon after Independence. If Peacock
Blue had had a jury they would have been Muslim. But the
judge and lawyers were Muslim, too, it turns out. Courts
can still be corrupt without a jury, though you only have
the lawyer or the judge to bribe or intimidate.

We all know there is much persecution in the world:
there were horrible crusades that had nothing to do with
the love of God, inquisitions that pitted Christian against
Christian, Hitler killed six million Jews, Muslims were killed
in Europe and now in Africa, Indigenous peoples the world
over have been massacred, minorities including Yazidis and
Christians are being killed in Iraq, Syria and Egypt. How
can we stop people doing this to each other?

COMMENTS

Affat I'm very sorry to hear of your cousin's sentence. It is so wrong. I'm collecting peacock feathers to put in a vase where I study at uni. The peacock is a symbol of renewal and patience and I will wear one to show I care what happens to Peacock Blue.

Crystal I'm sorry to hear that, Maryam. Even though I'm Muslim I disagree with Peacock Blue's sentence, and I'm going to wear a feather. That's a good idea, Affat.

Danyal This is the worst time to be a religious minority in Pakistan. We are all born free and equal but the reality is different. There are no fair trials and people are unfairly detained or given too high a bail to pay. There is violence under the blasphemy law and some are killed even before the trial. Death is the risk for campaigners against the blasphemy law, but the only way to reform the law is through mass awareness. Peacock Blue is my wife's cousin, so thank you, cousin, for this brave blog and petition. I have signed.

Rashid I can imagine how this girl feels. I do not believe my religion (I feel like I am locked in a cell too) but I cannot change it or I will be accused of blasphemy. If I do not go to the mosque with my father he beats me and I am nineteen! He continually watches me as if I am going mad and I know he is afraid.

Crystal That's awful, my family is Christian and when I became Muslim they accepted it. My mum even came with me to the mosque in Birmingham for Eid. I hope something works out for you, Rashid.

Tamsin I've got a peacock brooch of my mother's. I'll wear that for Peacock Blue. I think we need to respect each other's views, not try to make people the same as us, but allow them to inquire.

Ahmed That is called freedom of religion, which most countries, including mine, who are killing minorities have stated in their constitutions. They just can't seem to carry it out at grassroots level.

Maria We lost everything when my family fled the war in Syria. My parents even forgot our important papers.

Crystal Was that an attack on you because of your religion?

Maria It is war, they say, but Islamic State seems to be targeting our Christian towns. When our Christian village in Syria was attacked, there was fire everywhere. My parents thought we would survive if we did not flee. But my youngest brother was killed by a stray bullet. My mother has had a breakdown and now we live in a tent.

Affat It sickens me to see our great ancient religion undermined by this new harsh form of Islam.

Habib It is not new, sister, this is how it was meant to be. Who would want to change their religion if they were Muslim?

Maryam Habib, I could say the same about Christianity.

Fozia So, Maryam, you think Christianity is the best religion?

Maryam Everyone thinks their faith is the right one otherwise they wouldn't believe in it. They'd change. Well, if they could – sorry, Rashid, that sounds so insensitive. But this is not a forum to argue about which religion is best – but to air differences and breed respect.

Affat We can do something to help by signing petitions to stop ethnic cleansing.

Dana I live in Australia and I've never heard of ethnic cleansing happening since WW2. Are you sure you're not exaggerating?

Amir We've heard in Canada how Australia treats traumatised asylum seekers, so I'm not surprised you don't hear what's happening in the world. But you can easily find out on the web. Then you can give to charities and sign petitions.

Dana I don't sign petitions – someone may see my name on the list and bomb my house. If we let asylum seekers in we'll have cultural wars here. We don't want Australia ruined.

Tamsin Speak for yourself, Dana. There are many people in Australia who don't agree with the inhumane policies towards strangers. A country that doesn't look outside itself and help others in need will crumble on the inside. Let's do all we can to support freedom of religion and speech, and in the meantime, don't forget Peacock Blue.

Sammy You have a good blog, cousin, open to discussion, but not everyone is so progressive. It may be seen by the wrong people.

Maryam Bring it on – they need to see how balanced and intelligent people can discuss different faiths and still be allowed to retain belief in their own.

Sammy The people I'm thinking of are not balanced or open-minded. They are only a tiny percentage of our population but give everyone in our country a bad name. They shame us yet say they are protecting God's honour – but when has God needed our protection? We need his protection right now to save us from these thugs.

Maryam I think people confuse 'sticking up for God' for reverence and respect. I cringe every time someone at uni says ignorant things about my faith. But I don't throw grenades at them, for that would dishonour God too. At least my friends who are atheists respect that I believe. It's just old-fashioned good manners really. Kindness is putting ourselves in the shoes of others and realising what is important to them rather than to ourselves. The world needs to be kind.

MESSAGES

Sammy Ibrahim + 2 Maryam, could you send that petition to the Pakistani President? I think he has the power to stop the death sentence.

Hadassah Bashir Not for blasphemy, I shouldn't think. No one can override that thing. It's a monster that's alive. People here are calling it the black law.

Sammy Ibrahim Cousin, I meant what I said on your blog. These are very dangerous things you and some others are saying. Be careful. Extremist thinkers may not be commenting but will be watching. Glad you finally blocked Abdulla. We could Skype so I can tell you what it is like for us here.

CHAPTER

24

The first date in September for the appeal in the Lahore High Court was delayed. If only I could have gone to visit the judge for him to see the kind of girl I was, to disbelieve the 'evidence' on the paper in front of him. But it didn't work like that. Immediately, Mrs Jamal began planning her case for the next appeal date, even though one hadn't been set. It could take years, and I didn't have as much hope as she did for a reprieve, although Gazaalah told me a man was convicted by both lower courts for blasphemy some years ago and the Supreme Court let him free years later. She didn't say this to cheer me up, just to let me know it might have happened for others but it wouldn't for me.

She also said I should convert. For the first time I considered it. I'd be able to live with my parents again; we'd have to flee, but we'd be together. I'd see Sammy. I imagined myself hugging him, even though we were too old for it to be allowable.

Then reality set in. Wouldn't they execute me even if I did recant? It wouldn't save my life, it was too late, and I'd lose who I was. I couldn't bear the look that would be on Yesu Masih's face – the sadness, the betrayal. Couldn't I have waited a little longer? I resolved to stand with Him, no matter what the world threw at me.

The genie tossed the mail into the cell after breakfast. It was a letter from Rabia.

Dear Aster,

I am so sorry to hear of your sentence in court. It has been in all the papers, and no one I know has any sympathy at all. Sorry to mention that, but I want to say I do. You made me think more, and now you are paying for it.

I'm so sorry that I told Mrs Abdul that you had spoken about Yesu Masih, she got it from me in such a way I didn't realise I was saying it until it was out of my mouth. She's been so nice to me ever since but I hate that because of me you are on death row. I wish I had your strength. Though if you had become Muslim you mightn't be in prison now.

There are a few families back in your village and I have visited. They seem safe. The doctor you spoke about goes to a church in town. He sings really well, doesn't he? Just like a pop star on video clips. I pray for you, Aster.

Your friend, I hope, Rabia.

I couldn't think what her letter meant. How dangerous to go to a church. Just because her family was Masihi before, she couldn't convert back, or she'd be accused of blasphemy. Then she would be in a worse predicament than me. I couldn't even reply to warn her to be careful and tell her it wasn't her fault, for it could be read by an officer.

I also had to be careful – even Kamilah and Hafsah asked me what my beliefs were. Gazaalah laughed when I said we can all go to heaven if we accept that Yesu Masih died for us, but Muneerah's face turned dark.

'That's why you're in here,' she said, 'if you believe such crap.'

In this country if you thought differently about God you would be accused of blasphemy, and you could die.

That afternoon I wrote in one of my exercise books:

Being in jail for blasphemy is like being in a coma – everyone will go on with their lives while I lie here on my bed. Hadassah will have more children I'll never see. Sammy will marry someone else. It's strange how I used to think about Barakat. It's Sammy I think about in here – I hear his voice sometimes, telling me a funny joke. He always told jokes in Punjabi, it's a provincial language that's alive and funnier than Urdu, which is made from many languages. Now I think about dying when I never did before. I know what is written about heaven, yet still I feel confused and restless, on the verge of tears, and yes, angry that I'm here at all. Some days, facing death makes me appreciate it here – this is my cell, it's my home. I'm not truly afraid of dying but I am afraid of the hanging – what if I soil myself, will it hurt if my neck breaks, what will it feel like not to be able to breathe? But isn't that how Ijaz died? Didn't he die because he couldn't breathe?

I have learned too much here. I don't feel fifteen. I feel old, as if I have lived my whole life but just can't remember it. I am safe at least, although the genie beats me if I don't tidy up quickly enough or if I stay in my bed too long in the morning. I find myself wanting to please her like I tried with Mrs Abdul. Again, my reward is not to be beaten. There is no softening, and no smiles. In the night I often wish they'd get the sentence over with, execute me and be done with it. In the daytime I hope that the appeal will be successful.

More letters came. They always helped to stop my morbid thoughts.

Dearest Aster,

Greetings in the name of Allah and may he be merciful to you. We are thinking of you and daily hope to hear good news. We can't imagine how frightened you must be. If we could do something more for you we would. It is a deplorable situation that a child is kept in prison and for such a thing. Your cousin Samuel Ibrahim has visited us and we were very impressed with him. He has a plan for your benefit, we hope it goes well. We are thinking of your welfare as always.

Colonel and Mrs Rafique

I couldn't imagine what they meant about Sammy, so I opened the next letter. It was from Maryam in English and it made me realise what Abba had been trying to tell me about fear. To not fear doesn't mean we won't feel fear, but that we mustn't give in to it.

Dear Aster,

Our family is very sorry to hear of the delay in your appeal. I have 200,000 signatures now on the petition that people all around the world are signing for you. So please do not lose heart, the whole world is hearing about Peacock Blue.

If the High Court agrees with the Sessions Court ruling, then there is the Supreme Court in Islamabad. It has been known to override a High Court's ruling before. I have been in contact with your lawyer and she is very hopeful of a positive decision. She will be using the petition as part of her next defence. Surely the High Court will be beyond reach of the extremist clerics.

I had thought it would be easier than this, and you would be out of prison by now. Freedom and human rights issues are not as clear-cut as I thought in the beginning – they can mean different things to different people. Some people's comments on the blog are troubling, but I will keep it going so more people learn about you and what you're going through.

Nelson Mandela, who spent 27 years in jail unjustly, said, 'I learned that courage was not the absence of fear, but the triumph over it. The brave man is not he who does not feel afraid, but he who conquers that fear.'

Please do not give up hope. We love you dearly and continually pray for your appeal and release.

Your cousin, Maryam

Those hopes of appeal were soon dashed. One morning in January I woke up to breakfast and the *Dawn* newspaper. Karam had thrown it into the cell.

'See what good that stupid lawyer was? You'll get no special treatment now your guardian angel is gone. And good riddance too, with her high and mighty ways.'

I stared down at the paper in shock. What could he mean?

'What is it?' Kamilah said.

My heart beat faster as I climbed down to pick up the paper. On the front page was a full-colour picture of a young man with blood on his face, kneeling on the ground, weeping. In his arms he held Mrs Jamal.

'Nay. It can't be.'

'What? What is it?' This time it was Gazaalah.

'My lawyer has been shot.' A single sob escaped, unwilling.

Kamilah gasped, but Muneerah said, 'Well, that's what happens when people support blasphemers. She died because of you.'

I stared at her with my mouth open. I still couldn't take it in, yet slowly a wave of guilt and despair rose and swamped me.

Underneath the picture was an article.

'What's it say, girl?' Gazaalah asked irritably, but Kamilah gazed at me in sadness.

I took a breath. 'It says the Khan family will not let this go. Even though the country needs the blasphemy law to protect religious beliefs, they will work to help reform the law so it is just and protects minority groups.'

I stopped as Durrah snorted.

'No one can fix that thing,' she said. 'Look at you and Hafsah. You'll rot in here if they don't hang you first.'

I couldn't stop looking at the picture. Mrs Jamal had been shot outside her front door. *Her own house, where she should have been safe.* Further down the page there was a picture of Asia Bibi and how her High Court appeal had been rejected – not just deferred like mine, but rejected. Her death sentence was confirmed. What hope did I have now?

All day I stayed in bed. And the next.

The genie came in and beat me. 'Show us what you're made of, you stupid girl.'

I said to myself I didn't care if I was beaten but I did care. It was very effective. After it happened three times I made sure I was out of bed when breakfast came. I slept during the day but that seemed to go unnoticed.

Then the paper was tossed in again.

Karam said, 'You're in it, 753. Make the most of it – you'll soon be forgotten, no one will care what happens to you.'

He stared at me from the corridor, watching me as I climbed down from the bunk. I picked up the paper and retreated to my bed. I held my breath, willing him to go. Finally, he did.

'Be careful of him,' Kamilah said. 'Tell me what it is when you can.' She said it quietly and I nodded.

There was nothing about me on the front page. Coverage of Mrs Jamal's funeral would have been on the day she died. I turned the pages – maybe Karam was bullying me? – and found the piece halfway through.

Village is attacked following the shooting of a lawyer who was conducting a blasphemy case. Christian schoolgirl Aster Suleiman Masih has been given the death sentence for blasphemy and Mrs Jamal Khan was planning to appeal to the High Court in Lahore when she was killed.

There was no picture of the village but it must have been ours. Tears streamed down my face as I checked for anything else. The reporter had interviewed bystanders.

One man had said, *Blasphemy against Islam cannot be tolerated and the village was burned to send a message to Christians living everywhere. If you live in our country you have to be like us.*

Horrible, horrible.

Had everyone forgotten our flag? Since 1947 the white section had been a reminder that minority cultures were welcome here. And what about my relatives? Even though they were staying elsewhere, what if some had returned, what if the men had gone to work in the fields? Surely Rabia wouldn't be visiting. But I couldn't write to Rabia or her parents may see it. It would get her into trouble.

Then Karam was back at the door, standing there, looking at me through the bars. Jani saw him and fell quiet. All the women did too. I pulled my shawl closer around me. It should have been enough to make a decent man drop his gaze but Karam's didn't waver.

What had happened to make him like this? It had been touches and innuendos before, not this open crazed staring. I thought with a shudder how he was even worse than Ikram. He unlocked the door.

'The other guard is sick today. It seems I have to take you to your exercises.' His sneer told me what he thought of my privilege. 'Out you come, 753.'

I climbed down, my heart thumping, and took hold of Hafsah's hand. I didn't want to be alone with Karam. He reached in and grabbed me.

'Only you, 753, she's not a minor.'

I glanced at Jani as Kamilah drew her closer. I didn't want her near Karam either. I hoped there were other people exercising in the small courtyard, but when we arrived, chained together, the courtyard was empty.

'Can you unchain me?' I tried to keep the shaking out of my voice. 'Then I won't be a bother.'

His voice changed and became wheedling like Ikram's in the police cell that night. 'You won't be a bother if you do what you're told.'

He put his hand on my head and pushed down until I had to kneel in front of him, then he unzipped his fly. I smelt sweat and filth. I didn't know what he wanted and I felt disgusted to be this close to a man.

He chuckled. 'So you've never done this before. I'll show you.'

He pushed my head forward and I cried, 'Nay, nay!'

'Stupid girl,' he shouted. 'I was going easy on you, well, now you'll find out!'

He hit me across the face with his fist and punched me in the chest. I fell to the ground on my back. The chain on my arm pulled tight and I gasped. I thought my shoulder would be dislocated. My glasses were lost but I had no time to grope for them. Karam fell on top of me. There was a crack as he held my chained hand with the other above my head and I screamed. I tried to bite him but every movement hurt my chest and I couldn't breathe properly.

Hadassah flashed into my head. Did it start like this for her?

I screamed again, 'Yesu!'

But Karam slapped me so hard my head rang and everything felt mercifully far away.

Then I heard a noise, the door, someone was talking. I shook my head clear. His hand was on the band of my shalwar when I heard the genie.

'What is going on here?'

Karam knelt up and growled at her, my arm stretched forward on the chain, hurting my chest. I winced.

'Get out of here, she needs disciplining.'

The genie folded her arms over her chest. Behind her were Kamilah and Jani. I crawled as far back from Karam as the chain would allow. What would the genie do? Who was the higher ranking officer?

She didn't back down. At least she was bigger than him.

'I'm not going anywhere. I'm bringing this woman and child for exercise, since you didn't.'

Karam unlocked the chain and stood up.

'You'll keep,' he growled at me.

I'd never been so happy to see the genie but I wasn't silly enough to show it. I mumbled thank you through my tears without making eye contact, doing nothing to set her off.

She was just as likely to slap me for getting myself in such a position.

'You can wait here until I'm ready to take you back.' Did her voice sound less harsh? I still didn't dare look at her.

Without drawing attention I found my glasses and checked myself. My head hurt and my nose was bleeding, but apart from what I presumed was a cracked rib and the shame, I wasn't hurt. I closed my eyes and rested against the wall in thankfulness.

Free Peacock Blue

To see a world where freedom,
peace and justice reign

Sign petition <u>here</u>
Target: 250,000

Lawyer Murdered

A lawyer has been murdered for defending my cousin
Peacock Blue, while fighting for social justice. And I've just
heard that Peacock Blue's village has been attacked.

Who instigates things like this? Why does this sort
of thing happen and police stand by? Is any of this
acceptable? We have over 200,000 signatures now on
the *Free Peacock Blue* petition, but it didn't work on the
President. The justice system doesn't allow the President to
make that decision at this level of the proceedings. He has
to wait for the trial in the Supreme Court before he can
grant a pardon.

If someone else takes the case to the High Court I will
send the petition to them. Mother-of-five Asia Bibi's
appeal to the High Court has just been rejected and her
death sentence confirmed. There were 25 clerics in the
courtroom and 2000 outside. Two judges are needed
to override a death sentence but what if those judges or
their families have been threatened? If they don't override
the death sentence the rest of the world will criticise the
injustice, and if they allow her to go free, maybe there will
be a personal price to pay. I hope the petition is enough

to help free Peacock Blue. Find out how to write a letter to Peacock Blue <u>here</u>.

COMMENTS

Crystal It is in all the papers in Britain today. So sorry about all this trouble for your cousin and her family. I hope she is freed. But the whole thing has made my mother say she wishes I didn't convert to Islam, even though she saw it made me happy.

Habib They should just execute her and stop all the trouble. If they had done it straightaway that lawyer would still be alive.

Khalid That's a disgusting comment to make, Habib. What planet do you live on?

Affat Many lawyers are protesting in Lahore today over this injustice.

Shafique There is a rally in Toronto where I live too, for human rights and freedom of religion. I'll be there. With a placard I've painted of a peacock.

CHAPTER

❧

25

Karam had said I was forgotten, that no one cared about me. Maybe he was right about the last bit but I knew I wasn't forgotten. Gazaalah told me ten thousand men were marching to say I should die. The paper was shoved in my cell again to prove it.

But I found some better news in the middle: Malala Yousafzai had spoken at the United Nations on her sixteenth birthday. It lifted my spirits above the crowd of angry men shouting for my death to learn of a girl fighting for girls everywhere to have an education and to be treated justly. I imagined she was also meaning me.

Karam came to the cell. My rib hadn't healed yet and it still hurt to roll over on the charpai. Hafsah had let me sleep with her as it hurt my chest too much to climb. I never wanted to see Karam again. Surely he wasn't here to take me to exercise again – it wasn't the right day.

A frightful shiver swept through my body. I was already

hurt and I wouldn't be able to withstand him in my condition. But he stood there staring at me.

Hafsah put a hand on mine. 'Don't go,' she said. 'You can refuse – they'll just beat you.'

'He'll drag me out,' I answered, my rib hurting just thinking about it. He could hurt Hafsah too.

Karam unlocked the cell door and glared at me. 'You have a visitor.'

His sneer told me he thought it was someone I didn't deserve. Or was it a trick? I stood on the mat and he reached in for me and dragged me. It was the arm on the same side as my cracked rib and I cried out.

He grinned as he chained me to his belt. 'I like to know I've made an impression on a girl.'

I made sure there was no eye contact, did not encourage or incense him. He leaned down. I smelt his breath and almost gagged. 'You owe me something.'

I gasped. It was a trick after all.

'You give me something or I'll take you to the courtyard instead.'

What did he mean? What could I give him in the corridor, in full view of other prisoners? A kiss? I didn't think I could stand the humiliation. He stood watching me. I could tell I wasn't going anywhere unless I acted.

'What do you want?' I stumbled over the hated words and he rubbed two fingers together.

Money. He wanted money. Abba had given me some but I was keeping it for something important, though my virtue was worthy enough.

'I don't have much.' I pulled ten rupees from my qameez pocket. He stared at it so long that I expected a rebuff. He'd want more than that. What if the other forty didn't satisfy him either?

But he smiled. It was not a kind smile and as he took the money, brushing my fingers, I felt caught like a tiger in a trap. He handed me a piece of chewing gum. I didn't want anything from him but it felt dangerous to refuse.

His grin was loathsome, showing how he knew my money would run out. He'd have me one way or another and the longer he got to play with me, the better. I would never be free of him. All the way to the interview room I berated myself, but what else could I have done?

Karam unchained me at the door and didn't push me in or touch me. My reward for his little victory.

I walked in. There was a man sitting at the desk.

'Sit down,' he said.

I wasn't sure. I glanced back at Karam and was horrified to think of him as the safer person of the two.

'Do not be afraid.' The man indicated the chair opposite him. Was he an interrogator? Were they going to torture me at last? But why would they need to interrogate me? I already had the death sentence. I calmed myself and sat on the edge of the chair.

The man regarded me. 'I am Sarwari Asif Khan. I am your new lawyer.'

He had hollows under his eyes. I still didn't relax. If he was who I thought he was, he may want me dead.

'Are you Mrs Jamal's father-in-law?' I ventured.

'I am the father of Jamal, yes.'

Immediately a single sob escaped. It was happening a lot lately and I couldn't always stop it. 'I'm so sorry. You must hate me.' I looked up at him and saw his eyes change: they were troubled.

'No.' It was too loud and I flinched. 'We do not hate you,' he said more gently. 'But there are certain laws that need reforming.'

He glanced over my head, probably at Karam. Mr Khan was a lot like Mrs Jamal – I could imagine why they chose her for their family. He was fiery, passionate and strong. I couldn't imagine anyone killing him, but what if they did? Another special person gone because he tried to fight injustice.

'What is the matter, Aster?'

My eyes were brimming. Even hearing my name and not my number was undoing me. 'I don't want you to die because of me,' I managed to say. My mouth quivered as I attempted to control myself.

He stared at me for so long it was unnerving. Then he said, 'My son's wife did not die because of you. She died while fighting injustice in this great nation, to gain rights for everyone. She died honourably, as a warrior does in battle. Already there has been a softening in the hearts of more imams. She has not died in vain, dear girl.'

He was kind and it made me weep properly. I could always control it for Mrs Jamal. I dashed the tears away.

'You have been through more than most girls your age. My daughter-in-law always spoke of you as brave and pure. It is the highest commendation in our family.'

'I don't feel brave – much of the time I am scared.'

'Only fools are fearless, Aster.' He smiled at me then and I gave him a bleary one back.

'Now, I have carried on with the preparations that my daughter-in-law began in appealing to the High Court in Lahore. 'There is a petition on the web collecting many signatures for you. We will use that in the appeal. No doubt the appeal will take some time to be heard, and I will not visit you as she did. Just remember you are not alone. And you can call for me.'

He gave me a card with his phone number. I couldn't imagine Karam letting me use the phone or phoning my lawyer on my behalf. 'What will you give me?' he'd ask. Could I ask Mr Khan for money to save myself? He'd ask why I needed it and I'd never be able to explain.

'Aster?'

I blinked at him. 'Do you feel safe in here?'

I touched my side. Was Karam watching, listening? I gave the tiniest shake of my head and Mr Khan frowned. Then he glanced at his watch. It was made of gold.

'I have another appointment.' He stood and so did I. He came close to me and put his hand on my head in blessing. It made my eyes fill again, he reminded me so much of the Colonel.

'Keep strong, Aster, I do not know why God allows such things, but he is merciful. Remember this.' He left the room and I blinked my eyes free of tears so Karam wouldn't see them. I girded myself for the trip back to the cell as he chained me.

Letters came that afternoon, but they were from people I didn't know. *Should I open them? Would they be condemnations?* Gazaalah's comments were fresh in my head. Hafsah had never had a letter all the time I'd been there, so I gave her one to open. She had learned some words and could read a little now. Some letters were like form letters, typed, but still it was uplifting to read them; others were handwritten and weren't as easy for her to read, so I helped.

Dear Aster,

My name is Fozia and I live in London. I am very sorry that you are in jail for believing something. It would make me not believe but your cousin says things like this can make belief stronger. A lot of work is being done to get your sentence revoked. I have also signed a petition to free you and have shared it on Facebook, Twitter, Instagram and my blog. I hope you can keep strong. I don't think I could. There are hundreds of thousands of people around the world who know about you and want you to be released.

Best wishes, Fozia

The next we picked was in English. Imagine if I'd never learned English in school and with Ijaz – how would I have read it? Would the genie have sat down with me and read it aloud? This made me grin and Hafsah wanted to know what was funny. We laughed and I couldn't believe it.

'We're allowed to laugh,' Hafsah said, wiping her eyes, and I caught a glimpse of Narjis in the next cell. She was laughing too, even though she couldn't know what we found funny.

Dear Aster,

You don't know me but I heard about you on the web. I'm so sorry you are in prison for what you believe, for I imagine that's what it boils down to. I hope your appeal is successful and you are released. You could live with my family in Australia if the government would let you in, but they would make you do so much paperwork in Pakistan that you'd be in too much danger while you waited.

I'm learning how much danger there is for people in many countries. I never knew before. We don't have war in Australia or cruel laws for our citizens, just for people who come without a visa (sorry).

I haven't been through anything like you have but I know suffering produces perseverance which develops character and then hope. My father says we can get through anything with perseverance and hope. Here is one of my favourite verses: 'May the God of hope fill you with all joy and peace as you trust in him, so that you may overflow with hope by the power of the Holy Spirit.'

I am praying for you, I am your sister in Christ, Tamsin.

PS: Here is a peacock feather. A girl on your cousin's blog suggested

we wear a peacock feather to always remind us of you and if
anyone asks why we wear it we can tell people about you.

I picked up the feather and the Rafiques' garden swirled into my mind. I could even smell the flowers, see Neelum raising his beautiful tail for me. It made me weep. There were other letters, some from men and their families, even from children. There were more peacock feathers, and I had enough to fill a tin cup. This was the letter Hafsah liked best. It was written in Urdu.

Dear Aster,

I bring greetings from my family to yours. I am not Christian but I am Pakistani like you. I don't believe what some ignorant people here are saying: that people need to be Muslim to be true Pakistani. I am fighting for you to be free, by sharing petitions and speaking at university events in Karachi. This situation is wrong. You shouldn't be in prison.

In our nation Muslim, Christian, Hindu and other minorities have to stand together to keep a good life for us here. Be encouraged – there are thousands of Muslims, imams included, who think this also. Now we have to pray that the people in the justice system can be as brave as you, and release you. Allah is great.

Your Muslim sister, Affat.

CHAPTER

26

A friend of Mrs Jamal visited me. Her name was Zaib. For once I met someone in jail who was well named, as Zaib means beauty; she had the fair skin, light eyes and brown hair of a Bollywood actress. And she wore glasses like me, except she didn't try to hide them. Hers had big rims and were the same colour as her outfit. I wondered how many pairs she had.

'I am sorry to hear about Mrs Jamal,' I said after we exchanged greetings in the interview room. My eyes prickled, as I remembered the image from the paper. 'Her husband must hate me.' I said it regardless of what Mr Khan had told me.

Zaib was quick. 'It is not your fault. Her husband is a lawyer also and his father has a law firm interested in social justice and human rights. They will not give up.'

'What can they do?' I asked, without thinking how hopeless the words would sound.

Zaib didn't deny it. In her eyes was the same sad pity I had seen in Rabia's in Islamiyat class nearly two years ago. Instead, she took Mrs Jamal's notebook from her bag.

'I am a journalist and need you to write a story.'

The notebook was mesmerising. The last time I saw it Mrs Jamal was so full of life.

I blinked. 'What story? Mine?'

Her head tilted in affirmation and she waited.

It was too big. I felt the wings of fear flapping all around me.

'I understand your faith calls you to accept your circumstances and I've heard you are an intelligent girl. God has given you that gift, and strength, for a purpose.'

I raised my eyebrows; I knew this wasn't polite, but I couldn't help it.

She tried again. 'Do you want to stay in here?'

'Nay.'

'Do you want others to be treated as you have been?'

'Of course not.'

'You can help make sure they're not.'

'How will my story do that?'

'The more the world knows about prejudice and injustice, the less it can fester. Prejudice is a dung heap. It seethes with life when it is left alone. We need to dig this dung heap up, spread it over the ground for the world to see.'

I knew about dung. How many times as a child had I fashioned Gudiya's dung into chapatti-sized pats and stuck them on the back wall of our mud house to dry, ready for burning in the winter?

'Would people want to know?'

'Some do, others won't realise what is happening until we tell them.'

'What can it achieve?'

She paused. 'It's true it could be too late for you. You're waiting on the High Court, but since Mrs Jamal's father-in-law Sarwari Khan is handling your case now, it is possible that Maryam's petition will sway the court, show the world's displeasure about your treatment.

'On the other hand, it could help someone else. Reform could come.'

I thought of Asia Bibi still on death row after six years and the hordes of people who hadn't been accused yet.

'Aster, do you know that people all over the world are sending each other peacock feathers to show that freedom is important? One voice can start change, but other voices need to be raised also.'

I stared at her in shock. *All over the world?*

She nodded at my expression. 'The whole world knows about Peacock Blue.'

'Why are you interested?'

'I am a journalist. I love my country, my religion, my culture, but we need to do some house-cleaning.' She gave me a smile, but it was grim. 'We have mice in the cupboards. You know about that, I expect.'

I inclined my head, thinking of the mice that got into our sack of flour one winter. How I cooked rice with mice dirt in it without noticing.

'There is danger – not from the government, but from extremist groups if they realise you are writing about blasphemy.'

'The Taliban?'

She bit her lip. 'Such a pity that a group which began in order to bring justice is now acting unjustly themselves. They are calling for your execution as an example even though you are innocent.'

'In their eyes I am guilty.'

'A Christian will always be guilty in the eyes of an extremist. This is religious intolerance. Mr Khan knows the danger you are in and he will ask for you to be put into solitary confinement.'

I felt a sudden clutch in my middle. How strange that any change in my life felt dangerous. 'Why?'

'To keep you safe. From guards, other prisoners, anyone who would ask for visiting rights with the purpose to harm you. A female guard here also suggested it.'

The genie?

Zaib paused. 'When you are in solitary you will not be able to come to the interview room. I will see you at your cell but I will not be allowed to enter.'

My mouth gaped in horror and she tilted her head. 'I'm ashamed to say that some people who call themselves Muslims think it is doing God a favour to eliminate you. I'm sorry to speak so plainly but you do need to know the risk.'

'I don't understand why they hate us.'

'Not all, Aster. Please don't tar every Muslim with this

same brush. Have you heard of the Klu Klux Klan in the southern states of America?'

'Ji, we read *To Kill a Mockingbird* in school. Our teacher told us about the prejudice that lingered after slavery was abolished.'

'What did you think of the Klu Klux Klan?'

'They were evil.'

'Did you know they called themselves Christians?'

I stared at her, aghast.

'In your opinion, did they act in a Christian manner?'

'Not at all. Khuda says to love one another, not kill.'

She sighed. 'I fear we have the same problem.'

We sat silently for some time until finally I burst out, 'Where would I start? What would I write?'

'Start at the beginning – your life before you were accused.'

'The village? School?'

'Tell me about it. What do you remember before you were accused?'

I paused. It wasn't so hard to remember. 'The village. I was so happy, then something happened that showed me life wasn't a cornfield.'

'What was it?'

'My cousin was attacked by the landlord's sons.'

'Did your family get justice?'

'Nothing was done. They could have burned the whole village. It's happened in other parts of the country.'

Zaib was silent, then said, 'This is for the world, Aster. You will be surprised who is interested in you.'

'The world speaks English – I won't be able to write it well enough.'

I thought of Maryam and how she grew up in an English-speaking country and now she could write blogs for the world to read.

'Write it just the way you can, in Urdu if you like. I will translate it into English.'

'But my grammar ... My English teacher said I got my words in the wrong order. People would laugh.'

'I will be your ghostwriter.'

I frowned at her. *Ghosts?*

She smiled and patted my hand. 'It means I will fix everything so it sounds fine. No one will see me, and no one will laugh at you.' She took an iPhone from her bag.

'Let me show you something, Peacock Blue.'

She pressed Safari and a page appeared. The peacock painting from my Facebook page filled the screen. She scrolled down.

'Look.'

I leaned over.

Free Peacock Blue. A fourteen-year-old schoolgirl has been given the death sentence when world child rights rule that this is not permissible. Sign <u>here</u> to free Peacock Blue and save her from a death sentence.

Maryam's name appeared at the bottom. It was over eighteen months ago. I was nearly sixteen now.

'She's my cousin.'

'A very brave one.' Zaib regarded me. I knew what she

was thinking: could I be as brave? 'Maryam will post your story if you write it.'

'How? We have no internet here.' I shouldn't even have been able to see Zaib's phone.

'You will give the story to me. I will type it and check it, and when you have finished I'll send it to Maryam, then publish it as a book.'

I wasn't sure I had the energy. 'Won't someone wonder why I gave you pages?'

She leaned forward. 'Yes, they would, but I am now your English tutor. You are supposed to be getting training in here. Do you receive training?'

I shook my head.

'Now you will.'

She was a quieter version of Mrs Jamal. Both of them were intelligent, enthusiastic young women who cared about me, cared about people – from whichever culture or faith – who weren't getting a fair hearing.

I nodded at her, my eyes stinging at her kindness, making them heavy. 'I will think about it.'

Zaib handed me an A4 notebook. It had 'Exercises' written on the front. 'You will need to do an English exercise each day.'

She turned the book over. On the back was written 'Free Writing'. I opened it as I would an Urdu notebook and saw the blank pages. 'In here you will write your story. When I come next you will give it to me to mark,' she gave me a significant glance, 'and I will give you another exercise book to write in until I come again. In this way we will get your story out to the world.'

Still I resisted. 'It won't have a happy ending. There'll be no fine climax my English teacher used to talk about.'

'It still needs to be told.' Then she added, 'This is your life, just tell how it started, but write it for the world – they won't understand our culture unless you show them.'

'It will take a long time.'

I was surprised at how negative I sounded. Sammy would tell me to lighten up. He'd never let me get away with this complaining.

She pursed her lips.

'I don't mean to be flippant but you have nothing else to do. This may help.'

I wondered in what way she meant: to help get me out or to help me persevere?

When I returned to the cell, Hafsah was resting and so was Jani, and I thought for a long time. If Mrs Jamal were the sun, Zaib was the moon, a lesser light, but just as strong. It is the moon that keeps the whole earth on a steady path.

I opened the exercise book and picked up the pen.

I am a simple village girl, studying, helping at home, helping with harvest.

I crossed the first line out. What started it all? Mrs Jamal asked me that. She didn't believe it was Ijaz, but he was the bright star of my life – he showed me how to believe, not just to be a Masihi in name only, but a loving follower of Yesu Masih. When Ijaz died I felt like an orphan. But when Hadassah was attacked I first learned how precarious our lives were. If I wrote the story I could begin with Ijaz, for his death had changed my life the most, and then Hadassah.

School and Mrs Abdul could come later. I would never know if she just hated me for myself or because of my faith, or whether she truly believed the only way to force me to convert was to accuse me.

But I didn't want to convert – I had a relationship with Khuda through belief in Yesu Masih. If I told anyone that I'd be accused of blasphemy all over again. So perhaps I was guilty after all.

Yet Yesu loves Mrs Abdul and I have to forgive her whether I feel like it or not. Yusef forgave his eleven brothers for selling him into slavery and he turned his suffering into faith. Abba said if we waited to forgive until we felt like it no one ever would.

I turned the exercise book over and did an exercise, writing sentences instead. I still wasn't sure if it was worth writing my story. How could my words change anything? Every day I faced death, wondering if this was the day they would carry out the sentence – how would my story make a difference to that? Facing death did make me appreciate the people in my life. I looked over at Jani; she was napping in the next cell, her arm flung over the edge of the top charpai. 'You shouldn't be in here,' I whispered. No child should grow up in prison. What if this happened to my little cousins, or they were accused like me? They would be innocent but no one would believe them.

I decided then that, no matter how difficult, I'd write the story for them and all girls falsely accused; the Malalas and Mrs Jamals also, all those brave enough to fight for justice.

CHAPTER

27

There's a crowd of people shouting, calling out my name. But it's not like the mobs outside the courthouse. These are calls of love. Dada-ji, my dear grandfather, waves to me. I have never seen him stand so tall. A young man steps forward – he looks different but I know who it is. He is strong and well and he doesn't wheeze when he speaks my name.

'Aster, we are all here,' he says. 'Do not be afraid. This isn't your time, but when it is, we are here.' It is Ijaz.

When I wake I realise what Abba meant about our faith: I know that if I live for Yesu Masih, death will be my gain and it is true that in this instant, I am not afraid. Today I'm thankful for the life I've had. I have now lived a year longer than Ijaz, for today I am sixteen. And now I want to live for Ijaz as well.

Two years ago in March I was hemming my dupatta for high school and now I've just been moved to solitary confinement. This is not just a nightmare and I'm not sure how long I will be able to endure it. All the same, each morning when I wake up I force myself to be thankful that I am still alive.

This cell may be my future, unless enough pressure is put on the court system to execute me. The appeal to the High Court still hasn't happened. It's been delayed twice but I'm used to that.

I wonder if Asia Bibi is. She is waiting on the Supreme Court now. I would like to meet her but she is in a different prison a long way from here. I think about the journalist, Zaib, and the story she wants me to write.

I get the fountain pen and exercise book from my bag and write:

My name is Aster Suleiman Masih.

I smile – it's not a bad start. Maybe I'll write it as if I am telling Kamilah and Jani. They wept as I said goodbye when I was moved to solitary confinement.

I wonder if they will be allowed to visit. Jani said she'd miss my stories, and Kamilah thanked me for my love.

'You're like a sister,' she said. Hafsah cried too when the genie came to get me. I'll miss them all – maybe not Muneerah and Durrah, who said good riddance when I left. I'm still wary of the genie but I know now she has acted for my benefit.

My cell is smaller than the one I shared with Hafsah. It is also windowless like my other cell but I have a single char-pai that reminds me of my bed in the village. There's not much room for anything else except the hole in the ground to do my business; I will not be allowed to go to the bathroom to meet anyone who may hurt me.

I guess that means I won't have any exercise either, so I will have to pretend I am in the fields by walking on the spot. Narjis told me to enjoy the jungle in my new room. She may not be as unhinged as we think. Her eyes looked unusually shrewd the day I was moved. We survive as best we can. I have water in buckets, and my food is slipped in through a slot in the door. It's like living in the toilet.

The genie brings me the mail. This time there is a parcel and even though it's been opened, the contents look like they're still there. I say thank you and she comes into the cell.

'This is the last time I can do this. From now on only your closest of kin and lawyer can come in, and maybe the cleaner. No one else, do you understand? You do not need to be frightened.'

She's talking about Karam and I incline my head. I would never have been free of him if I wasn't in solitary confinement. It's a high price to pay for safety.

I look up at her and find her face is not as tough as I remember it, but I know she will still want to beat me if I don't get out of bed. She points to a corner of the ceiling.

'See that?'

I nod again.

'It is a camera. If anyone does get in here, they will be caught.'

Will they kill me first? I choose not to think that. I'm getting better at choosing what to think, and when I forget, I decide what Sammy would think. It only works if I'm well and when I pray. If I forget to pray my world looks grey. I wonder if Narjis prays to remember the jungle.

When the genie's gone I look in the parcel. There is soap, a towel, little bottles of shampoo, a brush, hair ribbons and clips. It's from a church in Australia, and I catch my breath to see the ribbons and clips. If Jani could come, I'd do her hair. Surely they'd let her in.

Then I read my letters. I'm still amazed by the mail from people I've never met. There are more from overseas but I read the family ones first. Even though we don't usually celebrate birthdays except for the first year, the little cousins have remembered mine and made cards. There's a letter from Ammi and Abba, and another from Hadassah. And then I see one from Sammy. I rip it open first. His greeting stops me short. He usually writes Dear Cuz.

Piari Aster

I hope you are not lonely. Soon I will be old enough to be able to travel to visit you. So far my parents are considering my safety. But what does my safety matter when you are locked in a cell?

I have been to see Colonel Rafique and he is looking into getting travel papers for you now while you are still safe, so they will be ready when you are released. I can't wait for that day and we all pray for this.

Also when you get out of prison, Uncle Yusef will pay for your flight to another country. There is a lot of support through the blog

Maryam has set up too. Some people are offering money for your new life when you get it. An organisation has promised to pay for your education when you are released and settled overseas.

France has already offered asylum to Asia Bibi for when she is released. I'm sure a country will do this for you also. You are an inspiration to so many and most of all to me.

I love you, I always have. I cannot remember a time when I didn't. Please let me keep writing to you and helping in any way I can.

Your devoted cousin, Sammy.

PS: I've been reading Solomon's Song of Songs, thinking of you. Remember, love is invincible facing danger and death.

The letter drifts to the floor and I sit transfixed. Now I know how Sammy loves me. Since Sammy and I grew up next door to each other, he was more like a brother and yet in here, he is the one I miss the most. His lightness, his laugh, his jokes always cheer me up in my head. I used to be so full of life, like Hadassah, but Sammy wouldn't recognise me now. I've learned to be quiet, to not provoke so as to avoid notice and a beating. I could be in here for years if I don't die. But Sammy loves me.

I pick up the letter, read it again. Then I read Abba and Ammi's. They send their love, hoping I can find space in my heart for joy. It's difficult for them thinking of me incarcerated, unhappy.

Am I unhappy? I was, but I am learning that happiness is an attitude, a state of mind and heart. I have my songs, my prayers. And my dreams. Yesu Masih has come in dreams whenever I needed a friend. What sort of miracle is that? How could I not believe?

I pray for a world where we are allowed to believe what we wish without fear, where we respect others' faiths and choices and don't kill them if they are different. I pray for a world where I can be free with Sammy.

That idea makes me think a long time. Then I pull the exercise book back onto my lap and write:

I was named after a Jewish girl who was chosen for her beauty and grace.

I feel a surge of power rise in my heart.

I will fight, like Maryam, like Malala. I will finish this story for my little cousins, for Jani and others, and maybe one day someone will be as brave as Shahbaz Bhatti, Salman Taseer and Mrs Jamal and manage to make reform.

When Queen Aster approached the Persian king to ask for her people to be saved from a cruel law that targeted them, she knew she and her people may perish. Yet she took the risk and moved the heart of a king.

I pray my story will also do this, and that I may walk this path, whether I live or die, to give honour to Khuda's name. Then, because I am alone I sing as I write.

I sing of hope, and I sing of joy.

Free *Peacock Blue*

To see a world where freedom,
peace and justice reign

Sign petition <u>here</u>
Target: 500,000
Write a letter to Peacock Blue

Peacock Blue's Story

Justice delayed is justice denied. Justice for Peacock Blue
has been delayed long enough. It has been two years since
she was sentenced at Easter time. Three years she has been
in prison – she's now 17. What comfort is it to us that no
one has been executed for blasphemy? What comfort
when other children accused of blasphemy have been
released?

The appeal to the district High Court in Lahore has
been postponed for the fourth time. At this rate it will be
years before Peacock Blue's case is heard, especially if Asia
Bibi's case is anything to go by. Asia Bibi's appeal to the
Supreme Court is still pending.

The United Kingdom MP for minorities is calling for
a reform to the Pakistani blasphemy law again. When a
church in Pakistan was bombed recently Muslims stood
guard with Christians against a further attack. During the
Egyptian revolution Muslims protected Christians during
worship and Christians made a ring around Muslims so
they could pray in peace. The world is changing, people are
growing braver. Join with me – whatever faith you have or
none at all – to help Peacock Blue see that change.

Peacock Blue is also fighting for change by writing her story. Not just to help herself and her family, but to show the world what is happening so others won't be wrongfully accused. Click here to download the full story.

The Truth about Peacock Blue

My name is Aster Suleiman Masih. I was named after a Jewish girl who was chosen for her beauty and grace from a harem of thousands to marry the Persian king.

Like her I belong to a minority faith and like her my life changed because of it.

This is how it happened.

GLOSSARY OF URDU
AND ARABIC (A) WORDS

Abu, Abba Dad

accha good, okay, I see

adda station

Ammi, Ummie Mum

ao come

Assalamu Alaikum (A) peace be upon you, hello

azan call to prayer

bahut very

Bara Din Christmas Day

bebekoof imbecile

beti daughter

bhai brother

burqa head to toe covering for women

busti small settlement, village or community

chai spiced tea

chana chickpeas

chapatti unleavened flatbread

charpai traditional string woven bed

chup quiet

chutti holiday

Dada, Dada-ji grandfather, dear grandfather (father's father)

Dadi, Dadi-ji grandmother, dear grandmother (father's mother)

degchi, deg huge steel cooking pot

dost friend (usually for boys)

dupatta a long silk scarf

Eid ul Fitr a religious festival to mark the end of Ramadan

imam worship leader of a mosque, officiating priest

Injeel New Testament

jai praise

jaldi quickly

ji short for yes; also used for respect after names or titles

jinn, genie a spirit, good or evil; can take human or animal form

kafir infidel, unbeliever

Kalimah statement of belief in Islam, the first pillar of Islam

kharmosh be quiet, shut up

Khuda God, usually used by Christians in Pakistan

Khuda Hafiz goodbye, may God protect you

lota jug

masalah containing spices

Masih Christ

Masihi Christian

mehndi henna

mullah Muslim religious teacher or scholar

naan flat bread made with yeast and cooked in the oven/ tandoor

nahin short for no; also nay and ji nahin

Nana, Nana-ji grandfather, dear grandfather (mother's father)

nay short for no; also nahin and ji nahin

neela blue

peelah yellow

phulkari Punjabi 'flower work' embroidery

piari dear

qameez long shirt or tunic

Ramadan the Islamic holy month of fasting

Sahib title of respect

salaam peace, shortened form of hello, usually used by Christians in Pakistan

shalwar baggy trousers

shalwar qameez outfit of clothes, long shirt and baggy trousers

shamiana marquee

sharam shame

shukriya thank you

tabla hand drum

teik hai okay, fine

Wa Alaikum Assalam (A) and upon you be peace; the response to Assalamu Alaikum

wah wow, wonderful

walima wedding feast or reception

Yesu Masih Jesus Christ

zarur certainly

zina adultery: sex with a man who isn't one's husband; includes premarital sex and rape if four male witnesses are not found to prove it was forced

NOTES

Asia Bibi, a Christian mother of five, is on death row for blasphemy in Pakistan.

Salman Taseer, the governor of Punjab province, Pakistan, was assassinated on 4 January 2011 by his bodyguard because he called for reform to the blasphemy law and tried to free innocent victims.

Shahbaz Bhatti, the minister for minorities and a Christian, campaigned to reform the blasphemy law and supported those accused of blasphemy such as Asia Bibi. He was assassinated on 2 March 2011 by Tehrik-i-Taliban Pakistan for being a blasphemer of Muhammad.

Acknowledgements

The Truth about Peacock Blue is a work of fiction and, even though a few public figures have been named, all characters in the story are fictitious and not based on any real person.

I thank Asia Bibi for her inspiring memoir, *Blasphemy*, so that we can know what is happening to her. I also thank Dr Ambrose Emmanuel for permission to use the words from his song 'Umeed' and Maria Farzeen for help with school dates and cultural details.

The phrase 'Changing the World One Girl at a Time' that Maryam uses on her blog is a slogan coined by the Walford Anglican School for Girls in Adelaide and used with permission. The concept of the fear of others corrupting our soul on Maryam's blog is inspired by Andrew Dutney's article, 'The fear of others has corrupted the Australian soul' at www.abc.net.au/religion/articles/2012/11/27/3642256.htm

Thank you, Lisa Berryman, who encouraged me to write a story for the UNICEF anthology *Reaching Out: Stories of Hope*, and also said (along with Jacinta di Mase) that my story, 'Just a Schoolgirl', would make a good novel.

Thank you to Lenore Penner and Gary Hawke for reading drafts. Thank you, Eva Mills, Sophie Splatt and the wonderful team at Allen & Unwin who helped me create this book.

ABOUT THE AUTHOR

Rosanne Hawke lives in rural South Australia. Many of her books have been shortlisted or notable in Australian awards; *Taj and the Great Camel Trek* won the 2012 Adelaide Festival Award for Children's Literature and *The Messenger Bird* won the 2013 Cornish Holyer an Gof Award for YA literature. For ten years Rosanne was an aid worker and teacher in Pakistan and the Middle East. She is a Carclew, Asialink, Varuna, and May Gibbs Fellow, and a Bard of Cornwall. In her books she explores culture, history, social issues and relationships. She also teaches Creative Writing at Tabor Adelaide. *The Truth about Peacock Blue* is her twenty-fourth book.

ALSO BY ROSANNE HAWKE

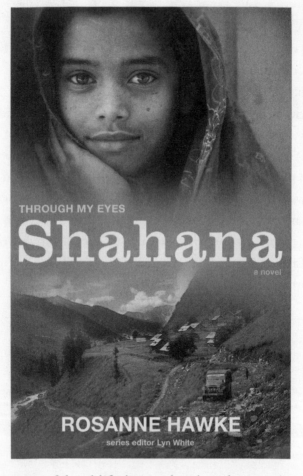

THROUGH MY EYES

Shahana

a novel

ROSANNE HAWKE

series editor Lyn White

'suspenseful real-life drama played out by appealing,
believable characters'
Katharine England, *The Advertiser*